About the Author

C. A. Miller grew up in a military family. She holds great respect for those who served their nation. Her father retired from the military, and the family moved back to Texas. She then attended Del Mar College in Corpus Christi, TX. After graduating college with honours, she moved to Southern California with her husband and children to pursue her career. It was during her time in California she attended USC's I.V. sedation course with her doctor at the time. Around 2007, her family moved to Las Vegas, NV. A resident of Las Vegas, NV, where she resides.

Dark Wish

C.A. Miller

Dark Wish

Vanguard Press

VANGUARD PAPERBACK

© Copyright 2024
C.A.Miller

The right of C.A.Miller to be identified as author of
this work has been asserted by her in accordance with the
Copyright, Designs and Patents Act 1988.

All Rights Reserved

No reproduction, copy or transmission of this publication
may be made without written permission.
No paragraph of this publication may be reproduced,
copied or transmitted save with the written permission of the publisher, or in
accordance with the provisions
of the Copyright Act 1956 (as amended).

Any person who commits any unauthorised act in relation to this publication
may be liable to criminal prosecution and civil claims for damages.

A CIP catalogue record for this title is available from the British Library.

ISBN 978-1-83794-315-9

This is a work of fiction. Names, characters, businesses, places, events and
incidents are either the products of the author's imagination or used in a
fictitious manner. Any resemblance to actual persons, living or dead, or actual
events is purely coincidental.

*Vanguard Press is an imprint of
Pegasus Elliot Mackenzie Publishers Ltd.*
www.pegasuspublishers.com

First Published in 2024

**Vanguard Press
Sheraton House Castle Park
Cambridge England**

Printed & Bound in Great Britain

Dedication

This book is dedicated to my family. Thank you all for being my inspiration and for always believing in me. With all the love in the world. Blessed be.

Chapter One
Present Day
Henderson, Nevada

The day started like any other day in the Nevada desert. Hot! It was the end of June, and the weather was already in the balmy low hundreds. Serena felt the heat radiating up from the earth below her feet, and this was only the beginning of the endless heat.

Another day of hell, she thought.

It wasn't in her makeup to deal with this kind of weather. This was her third summer here, and she planned to make it her last.

She craved cool breezes, shadowed skies, and lush green fields to walk barefoot in. Things not possible in the Mojave Desert, there were no green fields or shadowed skies, only unbearable heat. So much so that it felt like her skin was being cooked. She never understood how people could lie out in the sun for hours on end, tanning—no, cooking one's flesh to achieve that golden bronze glow, baking their way to skin cancer. Not that it mattered to her.

She knew how to take care of herself, she thought as she walked over to the medicine cabinet, reaching in for her SPF 205. She would definitely need it today.

Things had come a long way for their kind. Although there was, of course, quite a bit she missed from the old ways. Aspects this modern world could not offer. Things like the cold night air and no UV protective lenses were at the top of the list for her.

For her kind, there was a price to pay for this so-called freedom. Freedom that allowed her to walk under sun-kissed blue skies, as any human would. A price most found easy to pay, and for a while there, so had she. But now, Serena was full of doubt. Was it worth what had been taken away? Was this the civilization she'd dreamed of for her kind?

She knew what she wanted. What the immortal race needed. What they all dreamed of. The ability to revert back, revert back to what they had once been. Back to what their ancestors had once been. However, there was no turning back, not for her or her kind. Laws had long ago been set in place—namely, if any one immortal turned his or her back on the new ways, death would follow by the hands of the Holy Order. It would not be hard for the governing body to find out since every immortal was implanted with a microchip. No two microchips were in the same place. She did not even know where hers was placed within her own body. None of them did. So, there was no manner in which to dig it out of one's flesh.

To the humans, she was no better than the family pet, for they, too, had microchips implanted into their flesh. She'd been blinded for so long by the allure of what the humans offered that she missed out on her basic rights.

Rights so basic that every human had them. The right to hunt, to protect, and the right to marry. But she had none of those things. Much like the family pet.

Pulling herself free from her thoughts, Serena looked at the time—seven forty-five a.m. Time to go. Her shift would be starting soon, and she still had an appointment to keep. She jumped into her Camaro and headed for the 215 east. She hated this drive. Too many people in far too much of a hurry. Every single one of them not paying attention to what was ahead of them. Each and every one talking on cell phones, drinking their Starbucks, and applying makeup on occasion. She needed to reach 15 north toward the Strip. She hoped it would be smooth sailing from there to Sahara. The drive was so familiar that she could do it in her sleep.

She had to get to the Wine Barn in time for her daily treatment. If her treatments were late, her thirst would grow until she could no longer control it. She turned on the radio in time to hear one of her favourite songs— "Live Forever" by Soulidium.

"*It's time to die, so say your good-byes. Your mortal life is close to over.*"

She drove to the beat. She could always count on the radio station to play just the right song to start her typical, blazing hot day.

Before she knew it, she found herself at the Wine Barn. She parked her car in the usual spot on the side of the building, trying desperately to avoid the sun's reach. The Wine Barn sat in a sleazy part of town. Bums and drug dealers by the dozen lined the streets. Each one was willing to cut your throat for a dollar. Hell, who was she kidding? They would do it to look at them the wrong way. She saw them every day, hanging out in the alleyways, waiting for their next fix, next deal. The thirst in their eyes could not be misread. She understood that hunger. It was the same yearning she had, one that was life or death, and much more.

She loathed coming here. It always made her feel dirty. It started from the very moment she walked into the building. From the sign-in sheet to the clean white walls and the sterile smell in the air, it was enough to make her stomach tighten. Or perhaps it was the waiting in the lobby for a snob of a nurse to fetch her. To one of the many rooms with stainless steel tables and chains hanging from the ceiling, ready to be used. There was much to feel sleazy about.

Finally, a tall, middle-aged man in blue scrubs called her name with a look of contempt on his face. A look that spoke of his hatred. The loathing that ran deep within him. Serena followed without saying a word, silently stepping behind him down the long white corridor as the fluorescent lights flickered above them. Giving the sterile atmosphere the feel of a cheap, run-down motel. They stopped in front of room number sixteen. As he opened the door, the six came loose and swung upside down. She wanted to smile, to crack a laugh. For now, she was truly in a cheap, run-down motel room. All that was missing to complete the illusion were smoke-stained walls and rodent droppings lining the floors.

She stared at the tiled flooring, counting them to pass the time while she waited for the doctor to administer her treatments. She hated waiting in a tiny room for a doctor she did not know, for a treatment she needed. Serena was about ready to scream when the knock came at the door, and a young man popped his head around the door before entering the room.

"Hi, Ms. Serena Wulff. I am Dr. Toogood. I'll be administering your treatment today," he said as he pulled his light out of his pocket. "First, we need to do a few tests."

"I know! Can we get on with it? I have to get to work," she said, not trying to hide her distaste.

He was just doing his job, but today, she did not feel like placating anybody. She figured she'd better apologise for her behaviour.

"I'm sorry for snapping at you," she said in a much calmer tone. The calmness she did not feel.

He nodded his understanding as he continued to examine her. Serena waited for him to finish before she spoke next.

"Well, does everything look all right?" she asked as she watched him write in her chart.

"There seem to be some differences from your last visit," he replied, not even taking his nose out of her chart. "I do not think it's anything to become alarmed about. I am going to want you here for a few extra hours tomorrow. I would like to run a few more tests."

She nodded her understanding, not feeling it required more of a reply than she had given. She hoped work did not ask too many questions. Her dental assistant job did not care if you were mortal or immortal as long as you did your work.

"Well, let's start your session. Please, lie back on the table and try to relax. I would hate to have to use the chains on you."

She knew what was coming next: a series of shots—shots that hurt like hell. Like a liquid fire burning through her veins. Serena understood the reason for the shots. Why in God's name did they have to hurt as if hell's fire was running free in her body? This was different from when she had first started her treatments. Serena knew what was happening. She did not need the doctor to tell her what was happening. Her body was rejecting the serum. Rejecting what she had once coveted for so long.

She lay back on the cold stainless-steel table, and the doctor prepped her skin for the two stages of treatment. Three shots would be given: The first is a solution of liquid silver, not enough to kill, but enough to form a resistance. The second shot is an antibiotic to help combat the first, to keep the infection from starting. The last injection a pure UV liquid, developed back in the 1930s, is an injectable sunblock, if you would. Yet there was still a need for sunblock. Serena swore the treatments were meant to be a form of torture. One inflected by mortal kind meant to punish, to dominate. She thought about these things as each shot was given. Torture. Pain. Punishment. Dominance.

"All right, Serena, we're going to start the IVs now," he said as he looked her over. It was a look she never liked. It was part medical and part male instinct.

Serena turned her head and closed her eyes, dulling her senses as she waited for the blood to flow freely. Her hunger was great. It was a shame her kind was not allowed to feed as they were meant to. Modern laws had put a stop to it. What she would give to feel the first drops of plasma burst in her mouth as her fangs pushed their way through soft, warm flesh. As each drop of blood coated her tongue, her teeth and mucosa lining of her mouth had her body vibrating with yearning. These were the delicious thoughts that kept her company, which kept her sane.

Lying there as blood was fed to her, she thought about the centuries past. It was the only thing she had left of her old life. The law forbade anything that was of the old ways. For that life no longer existed—at least, not for her.

Her thoughts turned less and less self-centered as her hunger became manageable. That was all it ever was—manageable. Her hunger never truly vanished, always there under the surface, simmering, bubbling away until she felt the urge to drain a human dry. She did not think it would ever be gone again.

"All right, Serena, we're finished here. I expect to see you tomorrow," said Dr. Toogood, not even taking his nose out of her chart to look at her so she did not find it necessary to nod her understanding.

Serena stepped down from the table and walked out the door.

"Serena," she heard him call her from halfway down the hall.

"Yes, Doctor?" she said, hoping he would not call her back into the room.

"Make sure you stop at the front desk."

"Yes, Doctor."

She continued to walk down the hallway, mumbling to herself. Like she ever forgot to stop at the front desk. Not that anything they did was important. They just took her money and made the next appointment. All the while giving her a smug look of disgust. Envious of the fact that she would never age while they grew older with each passing year.

She needed to get out of the building before she went insane. She craved fresh air—or at least, as clean as you could get in Las Vegas. Grabbing her appointment card, she rushed for the door. It was the same for her after each treatment, always leaving her with anxiety. She needed freedom. However false it was.

She scanned the area before climbing in her car. A habit she had gotten into when at the Wine Barn. Each bum and druggie was a threat. Not to her. But her to them. Her hunger was not under control. It did not have to do with drinking blood but in the taking. She had to get to work.

Needing her mind taken off that particular hunger, she craved the distraction.

She made a beeline for the freeway. Needing to speed, to feel the wind brushing against her face and through her hair. It helped to take the edge off. However, speeding on 15 south was like being stuck in the Mississippi mud. You went absolutely nowhere. She could only hope the morning rush hour had passed.

Her cell phone rang. She hated her cell phone, and she hated talking on it when she was driving. Today, she was too aggravated to deal with it. Rolling down her window a little bit more, she looked at the face of the phone to see who was calling. *Work, great!* She didn't answer. She would be there in a minute or so. They could speak to her then. She already knew she was late. She did not have to be told of her tardiness. It kept ringing.

"FUCK IT," she said as she threw the phone out the window. One less item she did not need or want.

Horizon Ridge: 1 mile, the sign read.

Good, her exit was coming up. Exiting off the freeway, she turned right and then left. Work was just around the corner. She pulled into the parking lot in front of the office.

Time to work, she thought as she walked in. Hoping—no, needing the day to go by quickly, as the night called to her.

Chapter Two

Work went by with nothing major happening to delay her departure. Five thirty p.m., and it was as hot as midday. Making her way home was a fast drive, which she loved. When she stepped in, she relished the cold air as it hit her flesh. This was heaven to her. Making her way to the bathroom, she turned on the water, desperate to wash off the day of grime.

Most humans didn't take care of their mouths. You would be amazed by the conditions in which humans kept their mouths. Nothing surprised her any more. Not the rotting, decaying teeth to the pus-filled abscesses and the halitosis breath, caused by periodontal disease. To Serena, it was another day of work.

Stripping out of her scrubs, she let down her hair. The water hitting her body eased the tension of the day. She scrubbed her body free of the day's filth, imagining each bubble carrying away the infectious diseases the humans carried. The humans were tainted, no matter how clean and well kept. There was no avoiding it. One learned to pick and choose wisely. She shut the water off at the same time as her mind.

The darkness within her apartment gave her the chance to rest her eyes from the light of the sun to the unnatural fluorescents lights that graced the human world. Within her little dwelling, there was no need for protective lenses.

Opening her refrigerator caused her eyes to sting and tear up for the briefest of seconds as she reached for a pouch of B positive. She tore open the pouch and poured its contents into a glass. The aroma that filled the air was absolute heaven. A rich, heavy smell that would linger upon her lips for hours. She popped the glass into the microwave to bring the blood up to temperature, preferring to drink it warm rather than cold.

Lounging upon her bed, sipping from her glass, she watched the hours pass. A habit she got into during the summer hours. Hours prolonged by the summer days.

She dressed for a night out in a city that never slept. Sin City. Where the nightlife was as hot as the days. Nights sizzled with orgasmic, spice-filled aromas. A city where one had to be careful of one's date. Unlike most of her kind, she didn't like her dates to be drugged, not like the taste in the blood. The taint it left behind spoke of their drug of choice. A signature. She didn't walk the streets, searching for a willing soul. No. Clubs by the dozens hosted her kind. Like any other club in the city, there were ones not worth your patronage.

The night was young as she drove down the Strip. The sun was barely down, and the scum of the city already lined the sidewalks. Something always happened on the Strip, whether it was day or night. Not that the human eye ever caught it. Nevertheless, to her, they played themselves out in slow motion. Begging to be seen by all. The working girl was on her knees, earning a quick fifty bucks the only way she knew how. The john in the alleyway, pushed up against the wall, his head rolled back, eyes closed. Hands on the prostitute's head, holding her in place as she bobbed up and down, working his shaft. Licking. Sucking. Rubbing his sac, all to work the john into shooting his load. Trying her hardest to get to the next john before she needed her next fix.

A city that did not want to let go of its dark secrets, secrets held tightly in its grasp. Skeletons are better off left lying in the gutters with the miles of strip club fliers. Handouts are more like porn than advertisements. Porn promoting some young woman, desperate for a quick bill. But there was nothing new about this. Sex. Lies. Sins. That was what made this city, what ruled this city. Even in these modern times, sex, lies, sins, and cover-ups still rule.

To some, it was paradise. To others, it was a living hell. Hell they could not make themselves leave or escape. A never-ending nightmare, trapped by their own addiction.

The Strip was like a parking lot, traffic at a standstill, and Serena couldn't take it any longer. With too much temptation walking the streets, she turned into the nearest parking lot. Walking would get her to her destination faster.

Within five minutes, she found herself at the front doors of the Velvet Wings. A very high-class establishment any immortal worth their weight in gold frequented. This was the place to be and be seen.

She made her way to the bar for a much-needed drink. The barkeep flashed her a fanged smile that would've charmed the pants off any weak-minded woman.

"Good evening, Serena. What can I get you this fine evening?" he asked as he gave her a once-over. "You're looking exceptional this eve," he said with a smile hinting at what he wanted.

"Good evening, Rick. Thank you for noticing. Can I get a blooded wine?" she asked, smiling wide, baring her fangs.

He nodded his understanding and poured her a drink from the redhead on tap. She took a sip of her wine and scanned the area around her.

Her gaze settled on a tall, blue-eyed blond in the far corner, next to the orchestra. Extremely good-looking with an air of confidence. Confidence that spoke of his impact on female senses. The type of man human females flocked to, not caring if he was good or evil.

There was no harm in looking at him, in letting her eyes roam over his six-foot- five frame. In letting herself daydream about him pleasuring her body. His presence urging, demanding you took notice. His deep forest green eyes pierced to the very core of her being. She knew she could get lost in those eyes. Pulling her gaze from those mesmerising green pools as she continued to study his features. High cheekbones, to his aristocratic nose, full lips and chiselled jawline. His was a body designed to pleasure a man or woman. One that would awaken any hot-blooded woman's core with simply a look.

His black tux fitted to his body, showing off his muscular physique and he wore it well. This was no rented tuxedo. No, this had been made for him. Broad at his shoulders and tapered down to his slim waist. Her eyes paused at his waist. He moved his elegant hand and unbuttoned his jacket with his long, agile fingers. As if he meant to give her a better look. She raised her gaze to his in time to watch him arch his brow. His knowing stare and the smirk that now graced his beautiful face only added to her interest. That was as far as it went. Interest. Intrigue. Fascination.

The knowledge of his immortality magnified her uneasiness. She wasn't up to having sex with one of her own, not this evening. Immortal coupling was an extremely sexual, violent act, covered in blood. There had once been a time she would've jumped into bed with this man and shared in the passion she craved. Something had changed within her, and nothing was helping her. Needing to run free, to feel free, however short-lived. However false it was.

Finishing off her drink, she tipped the barkeep and headed for the door. Turning with a sigh, she took one last glance around the club. Her eyes stopped at the pool table and the couple playing. They seemed to pet and tease each other at every moment. She could feel the sexual tension between them. That same sexual tension ignited all around them.

What she would give to feel the same as the rest of them. To find some willing soul to seduce, to sweet-talk into giving up a part of themself. To feel their body pressed close to hers, to have their heat engulf her. Hear their pulse pounding in her ears. To have these changes in her stop. With that thought, she slammed the door shut behind her. Effectively closing them and her thoughts off.

She made quick work of the walk back to her car. Recognizing where she wanted to go, the only place she was free to walk in the woods, under the moon—Mt. Charleston. She found herself going up to visit her friends not only for the company but also for the freedom it gave her. They were the first two humans she considered friends. The instant she met them, she remembered thinking how much in love they were. She could see it radiate from them. At that moment, she knew what their future held for them. One filled with love, laughter, and the sound of children playing. All this before death would claim them.

What she envied the most, was near the end of their short lives, death would follow. While she might have love, laughter, and even children, she would never have death. Death, was the one peace she needed most of all. Dying was an illusion to her. For the briefest of moments, she'd live her life through their eyes. That was all it would be. A brief flash in time. She'd watch as their lives played out. Observe as they lived and as death slowly claimed them. They were not the first she would witness die, nor would they be the last. She desired eternal rest to claim her; it offered the freedom this modern life didn't, freedom from her current captors.

The drive to Mt. Charleston was short—too short for her liking. The quiet ride allowed her time to breathe. Time to replay the events of the day. Just one thing kept replaying itself: TEST. That was the last thing she wanted. Serena knew by going to see her friends, she wouldn't make her appointment. Not that she intended to. There would be no more testing of any kind for her.

Turning down the dirt driveway, she saw the lights flicker on. It seemed apparent at least one person in the Heffernan household couldn't sleep.

"Serena, what are you doing here at this hour?" asked Kimmie with a smile on her face.

Really not caring about the hour, Kimmie was always happy to see her friend. But Kimmie saw something different in Serena that night. Weariness. It ran deep within her.

"I had to get away from the city. I'm sorry. I should have called first," she replied with a look that spoke of her fatigue.

Kimmie understood the exhaustion her friend felt. To be controlled for eternity by human laws. Laws imprisoning her with the illusion of freedom. Laws Kimmie would never be able to handle. Knowing some strange person tracked her every move. It was a major invasion of privacy. A strange man on the receiving end of a computer, monitoring your every heartbeat so to speak.

As they made their way inside, neither talked, instead enjoying the perfect silence. Each lost in thought.

"So, what are you going to do, or are you going to stay up here forever?" She got up and went to the kitchen as she waited for Serena to answer her.

"I'm planning to go into the woods for a midnight walk. Maybe get lost under the stars. Until happiness finds me," she replied with a sigh.

"Well, care for a drink before you go? I got some fresh type O in this morning, or do you prefer B? I have some of that too."

Serena looked at her with a question in her eyes. What reason would her friend need blood? "Why do have plasma? Tom and you do not need it," she said as she stood and walked over to her friend, scanning her neck for marks upon her flesh.

"No, we have not been bitten. I had a feeling this morning that we would need it. So, I called the Wine Barn II and had them bring over supplies."

Serena did not need to ask what the Wine Barn II was. It was one more clinic, hidden under a different name. If a human ever went in, which many did, all they would see was assortments of wine and hard liquor. The store was a front for what really took place behind closed doors. If they ever went farther back, their eyes would be opened to the dark secrets, which lay under the surface. Alcohol was the only legal way to pay for the clinics. The clinics only received ten percent of government funding. The government did not ask, so they did not tell.

She found it odd they would deliver supplies to a human. What on earth had Kimmie told them? To her knowledge, they did not supply to humans. While humans knew about her kind, they did not know how they got their blood. The government and the immortals alike liked it that way.

If the humans actually knew how the blood was collected, they would want no part of her kind. Blood banks were more like blood farms. People were invisible to society, the souls that lived in the shadows of the streets. The men, women, and children you didn't see, even when they were in front of you. Abandoned bodies bought from hospitals. Patients lost to comas and their families had given up hope. Kept alive by machines for a constant supply of blood.

"Here you go. Drink up. See you in the morning. I need to get some sleep. Another midnight craving," She said as she rubbed her baby bump. "Good night," she said as she kissed Serena on the top of her head.

"Sweet dreams, sweetie," she whispered, watching her friend waddle off.

Seven months pregnant with twins, and it made her even more beautiful. She knew Tom must be busting at the seams with happiness, and she couldn't blame him. He would be a wonderful father. No doubt about it. Tom was a man of honor, compassion, and in this century, that was non-existent.

Integrity and compassion were something not bred or taught in this modern world. All that existed were falsehoods. Betrayals, mingling together with what little truths were told. They were both one of a kind among her friends. She didn't have a great number of friends, but the ones she had were all honest. Honor was important in her friends—a quality that was a must.

From the kitchen window, the moon shone in, in a sea of silver. It looked close enough to touch. Yet hung high in the sky, out of her reach. It was one of the things that had ruled her life in the old lands. She'd love to be ruled by the night once again. To fully feel the moon's rays on her flesh without the city smog lingering between them. Without the noise of everyday life flooding in at every turn she took.

Kimmie & Tom,
Went out for a midnight walk in the woods.
Won't be out long. Need to feel free for a moment.
See you both in the morning.
Serena

The year had been hard on the woods and its inhabitants. The creek was dry, as was the brush. All would be healed with winter's arrival. Rain showers and newly fallen snow give the woods time to heal. She'd love time to heal from all the damage done to her body, trying to fit in with the humans. Winter called and, along with it, hibernation.

A flicker of light caught her eye, light out of place in these parts of the woods. Not that of a flashlight or a lantern, that of a flame. Her eyes must have been playing tricks on her. Then, she saw it once more. Maybe someone was injured and in need of assistance. Walking toward the light, she scanned the area around her, in search of anybody unable to scream for help. The fresh smell of blood would grab her attention.

Nothing. She couldn't hear or smell anything. The light got brighter, the closer she got.

"Is anyone out there?" she shouted as loud as she could.

She waited for someone to respond. Any little sound would catch her attention. No answer. Moving deeper into the darkness of the woods, she kept calling out, in hopes of them hearing her. She prayed she was not too late to help.

Serena was almost on top of the light source now, still, there was no one to be found. She was now face-to-face with light so bright, it about blinded her, unable to find the fire or any reason for the light to be here. She scanned the area around her, finding herself in the middle of a clearing.

The light dimmed as if a mountain blocked it out. Which was impossible because she was on the mountain.

Whirling around, she saw a man who looked as surprised to see her as she was to see him. In the blink of an eye, he was gone.

Her mind was playing tricks on her. It was impossible for him to be real; no man was built like him in the modern day—at least, not without the help of some serious use of steroids. Was she that horny, that sexually frustrated, that she was making up men in her imagination? It had to have been a mistake, a trick of the light.

Clearing her head, she watched as the light faded to the size of a small jewel. Moving closer, she saw it was more than a jewel, but a blade. Serena had never seen anything like it in all the years she had lived. The dagger was out of place. It did not belong in modern times or this country for that matter. She rubbed the blade's edge, testing the steel sharpness, not thinking the blade's edge would be sharp until she felt her blood flow free on her flesh. She gazed at her fingers, then at the dagger in question.

The edge of the steel glowed where her blood now touched. The dagger hummed and vibrated in her hand, sending chills throughout her body. Serena was unable to take her eyes off it. Rays of light shot off so bright that she couldn't see. She tried to let go, finding herself incapable of opening her hand. One minute on solid ground, the next falling. The light surrounding her was gone, replaced by darkness once more.

Chapter Three

Seumas couldn't believe what was before him. She could not be real. Oh, how he wanted her to be.

Neither of them said a word. Standing there in complete shock at one another. Looking each other's bodies over with a hunger that ran deep within them, a hunger that charged the air between them.

Each one trying to understand how the other had gotten there.

His nostrils flared as he took in her scent, desperate for the smallest hint of her. Dropping his blade, he reached for her, but she was gone. Just as quickly as she had appeared, she disappeared. Vanished from his sight and him within a blink of his eye.

He had only seen her for the briefest of moments. That was all it took for him to want her. His body grew hard with yearning.

He had been too long without a woman to see such a vision and not react to her. His wife—may she rest in peace—had been slain in her sleep by his enemies. They had been wed for two seasons and were expecting their first child. They were both very young and so in love. When all was taken from him one fateful night, the very moment he put his wife into the earth along with his unborn child. He had failed as a husband and a father, all in one eve, and it had broken something inside of him that had yet to heal.

Ten long years had passed since that dark night so long ago. He had not remarried or held interest in any one woman. Not dare to love, mostly out of fear that it would be taken from him once more. However he did not abstain from taking a lover into his bed when the mood struck. Which was few and far between.

He spent his time perfecting his craft, magic that ran deep within his blood. Passed from parent to child. In his case, from uncle to nephew. His mother and father had both been killed by the plague that spread like wildfire throughout the village. He was the only survivor. The day his uncle had found him, filthy and half-starved, he had realized he still had family. That was long ago, and he was not a child any more.

The only thing in his life he could count on was his magic. It had served him well the past few years, his country at constant war with itself. Clans fighting over land and women, clans that wanted more. Never satisfied with what they had. He couldn't criticise or put shame on any of them. He himself was guilty of the very same act. In fact, the very night his wife and unborn child had died, he had been warring with neighbouring clans. Trying to gain more land to increase his holding. That was the last time he warred against his fellow clansmen. The very moment he had found his wife and unborn child dead, everything else had ceased to matter.

The memory had been his constant companion—until now. Now, all he was able to think of was the woman who had appeared before him. He welcomed the thought. Relished in it. Wanted more of it.

Night fell and, along with it, emptiness. His day was no exception to the very same barrenness he felt. It accompanied him in his duties. There was much he needed to take care of before he left in search of the crystal. Duties to his clan took longer than he liked, but it was his responsibility, so he did it willingly. On the morrow, he would begin his journey.

No quick slumber claimed him after a long day's work. The night wore on, holding on to every second. Seumas lay in his bed, listening to the crackling of the fire. The popping of the flames sent pieces of ember up in the air, lighting the way to the heavens. Sleep was slow to welcome him, one last form of torture.

His dreams ran rampant within him, dancing about in his mind, playing out in a whirlwind of visions, but they were different somehow. Changed. The haunting stopped. Fogged memories gave way to new ones. Ones of a woman he did not know of or if she even existed. It did not matter if she was real or not. The simple fact of the torment he felt for the past ten years eased since he had seen this unknown woman. It was a foe he could not fight, nor did he want to. Maybe now, it was time to move on, to let go. To forgive himself for past wrongs, wrongs he had convinced himself of committing. Seumas prayed this was the case. Hoped the quest for the crystal was the start of a new beginning. A new beginning he hoped would end with love.

The crystal lets the beholder see the innermost truths in a man's heart. He knew it was not to be taken lightly. He wanted to love again. It was more than the love he sought, but hope. Hope seemed to be a fantasy to him—something he needed to find.

Day approached. No better time to start his quest. Throwing his bedcovers aside, he got out of bed and stretched the aches from his body. His bed chamber was quiet, as was the rest of the keep. Reaching for his tartan, he threw it across his body, not caring if it covered or not. No soul was up, so no need to cover up what would not be seen. There was a cool loch outside his keep that he intended to use as his bath.

He walked out to find his men sleeping on the ground by their horses. Apparently, they were planning on going with him, no matter what he said. He didn't know whether to be amused or angry. Amusement gave way to a smile.

Stopping at the edge of the water, he watched the mist roll over the loch. It danced upon the water's every ripple. Movement so slight that it was hard to see if one didn't look with unwavering eyes. With eyes that sought the calmness the water offered. It was a shame he was about to disrupt the glassy surface of the water. A moment in which the water's ripples would break the smooth surface of the loch.

The coldness of the water caressed his heated flesh in a fashion nothing else could. He felt the energy channel into his body. The water was a part of him, and it fed him in a method only raw energy could. He felt revived, body and soul. He swam for the embankment, only to be met by his men, mounted on their horses, awaiting him.

"MiLord, we're ready to ride out with ye," said William. He hid his smile, knowing well his lord was not overjoyed. His friend did not like his men openly defying his orders. In fact, it was never done, as all held respect for him.

"I do believe I made it perfectly clear. Ye are not to come with me. I don't like having to repeat myself."

"Aye. MiLord, we understand yer orders. We do not feel it prudent for ye to be without one of us at yer side," replied William. He knew well enough what Seumas would say, so to beat him to the punch, he would make the argument for him. "Before ye start to dig in yer heels on the matter, all we ask is one of us go with ye and the rest of us stay to do as ye wish, milord."

"All right, William, ye have made yer point. Ye will go with me. As for the rest of ye, since ye feel it necessary to be up at this ungodly hour, go tend to yer duties."

"Aye, milord," echoed across the lower bailey.

He watched as his men scattered across the bailey to do as their lord had bid. Within seconds, the field was clear and quiet. He finished dressing as he watched his friend prepare his horse. A task he had planned to do himself. He could see William was not going to allow him to do work he felt was beneath him. He would need to have a talk with him.

"Come, William. Time to go. We have a fair distance to travel today. I have a notion of where the crystal might be. No better place to start."

"Aye, milord, I'm ready to ride." William had not seen his Lord so eager in a very long time. Desiring nothing more for this quest to bring his friend the peace he so desperately needs. Although he wished it would bring a great deal more.

He watched as Seumas mounted his horse and motioned for him to follow.

Seumas felt more alive than he had in a long time, and he did not know if it was due to the journey or the woman he had seen earlier the previous day. All that mattered was, he did not care. He felt alive. Felt truly alive for the first time in a long time. Perhaps, this time, he would find the crystal.

They rode quietly away from the holding, each one lost in thought. Each one having more to think about than just the crystal he sought.

Chapter Four

Confusion took hold of Serena—a feeling she did not like. Endless darkness surrounded her. She felt like she might never feel solid ground beneath her feet again. Hours elapsed, yet felt like days to her. A sudden spark of hope flared within her; small orbs of light floated into the blackness, slowly lighting up the dark emptiness around her. Thankful for the light, she let out her breath she had not realized she held. While a creature of the night, she preferred the nights lit by the full moon. To have the moonlight caressing, reflecting off her skin, and to truly be the predator within.

Once again blinded by light, her eyes adjusted to the brightness. Her feet touched solid ground, and she jumped for joy from the mere feel of it. Smells came rushing in on her all at once. The dew on the grass and the scents of flowers filled her lungs. Sounds collided against her eardrums. Pounding their way to her inner ear and thousands of stored memories.

There was something different about her surroundings. This was not Mt. Charleston. Where was she?

Serena scanned the area for any hint of where she might be. A street sign would be helpful right about now. As luck would have it, nothing, just the surrounding beauty. She walked, not caring which way she went. Sooner or later, she'd run into somebody. Not caring much if she found another living soul, she was free. Serena could feel her body reacting to that very freedom. How could it not? It was so beautiful here. You could say it was heaven's playground. The gods had made this land for themselves.

She walked in peace her environment granted her a freedom she hadn't felt in a very long time. Listening to the sounds around her, taking in every rustle made by the wind. Wherever this land was, it held more wildlife than all of Nevada. Overwhelmed with the splendor and nature of it all, she couldn't walk any farther. She picked out a spot, taking in the magnificence of the land.

Serena watched the rolling countryside with unwavering eyes. The shades of green dancing among the land were like none she'd ever seen in all of the United States. Time gave way to new shadows, shadows darkening even the lightest of greens. There was a mystical quality about this land, and somehow, it was familiar to her. Serena did not fully understand how she knew this place, but she did know it. It would become clear to her.

The night mist rolled in, along with her hunger. The microchip within her body tugged at her self-preservation. Would the chip report back to her captures? She did not know, nor did she care. She needed to feed. Feed the part of her that was always hungry.

Serena headed into the woods, needing the cover the dense foliage provided, protecting her from prying eyes. She did not see any living soul for the time she sat, watching, but she was not willing to risk her life. She would hunt for the first time in many moons. Life in the modern world was one of leisure. In which hard work had lost its meaning. Today, for her, had brought back the true meaning of working for one's supper. Which was something she had not done in a very, very long time. It would come back to her with time, she hoped.

Not long into the woods, she discovered the secret it held. A pond that shimmered silver upon its ripples. Ivy and flowers entangled with one another, weaving a protective blanket around the silvery water. Serena moved closer to the mysterious water eager to get a better look at the majestic sight. A faint glow peeked through the muddied earth, tempting her. Calling to her.

There was weariness within her. She had already touched the blade. And look what had happened.

Despite what had happened to her, there was still a small part of her curiosity that wanted, no demanded to know what was hidden under the muddied earth. Pushing past the weariness, she entered the unknown. The water was deep. She hiked up her gown as far as she could. It wasn't enough.

Wading back to the embankment, she let her gown fall. The fabric's edge of her gown gently swayed in the water, a quick zip, and her dress slipped from her body. The frigid water felt much colder than it had moments before. Serena could think of one way to deal with the crispness of the water—dive in.

She pulled her body through the water with a grace that came all too easily to her. The glow was so close that she was almost able to touch it. Serena reached for it as flashes of light flicked quickly, reminding her of a strobe light in one of the clubs on the Strip. Her hand wrapped around a crystal. Thoughts, deep thoughts, feelings she never wanted to feel, came bubbling back to the surface. Feelings she kept locked away from her everyday emotions. Thoughts, if pondered on a daily basis that would drive her insane. Drive her mad beyond any point of reason. She not only felt her emotions, her own thoughts. She also felt the emotions and thoughts of others. Feelings so deep that a person would not know they lay within them. Not without doing some serious soul-searching.

This crystal was pure magic, and in the wrong hands, damage could be done. It was not for her either. It was better left alone. To make sure it would be safe, she placed it back on the pond bed and covered the crystal with the muddy earth. Satisfied the stone was fully covered, she pushed herself to the surface of the water. The cool night's breeze felt refreshing on her damp skin. Her hair clung to her body, offering her coverage, but did very little of that. Not that her bra and panties granted much more.

Becoming more aware of her body, she realized her eyes did not burn, which she found very odd. Serena was unable to recollect a day her eyes had not stung in the past years. No matter if it was day or night, there was always a constant pain, however slight it might be.

Needing to dry off from the chill of the water. Too bad she didn't have a warm towel to wrap around herself. Wringing her hair dry, she slipped back into her gown, praying her bra and panties dried quickly.

There was much more to occupy her time. It had been too long since she had last hunted for food. Doubt ran through her for the briefest of seconds. However brief, there was still doubt. Had the century of living in a modern world changed who she was? Wanting to believe the creature that lay dormant within would awaken from the century of hibernation, slumber that kept the demon at bay. But she needed that other side of her to awaken, it had been asleep for far too long.

Serena stood motionless, clearing her mind to reach a level of awakening. Awareness she felt necessary for her to hunt and feed as she once had, no longer able to be that mindless creature she once was. Time elapsed as she waited for her senses to be at their most heightened. Once she reached this point, she would be able to sense even the smallest of animals.

The winds carried a scent, causing her to open her eyes. A smell she had not tasted in years, perhaps centuries. It sent her blood running hot. Her pupils dilated in her excitement. This sensation was new to her, not remembering this awareness when she was young. That did not mean much. For it was a different time, a different place.

Her body flew through the woods. The wind caressed her face, surging through her hair. This was the freedom she had wanted. In the back of her mind, the thought of her microchip lingered. How would she be able to feed? She knew the answer, and it stopped her right in her tracks. She was hungry. However, she was not ready to hang herself over that hunger, not yet. She needed to find out where and when she was. For all she knew, the government was performing a test. A test she did not intend to fail.

Hunger consumed her, and Serena didn't like the fact that she was going to starve. Before that happened, she had to find civilization. Perhaps that would give her some idea of her whereabouts. If she was going to go without food, at least she could locate shelter. She could head back to the pond, but there was not much there to make any form of shelter. Serena kept pushing forward. She was bound to run into a cave, maybe even get lucky and find an abandoned cabin.

Dawn approached, and with that came the sun. The sun did not hinder her, yet no telling when that would happen. Without her daily treatments and UV protective lenses, how long would she be able to walk freely among the humans? This put her in grave danger. Especially now. Well, she wasn't going to think about it too much. Nothing could be done at this point.

Just when she thought she was going to sleep under the stars for what little longer they were out, an old barn came into view. The outside and inside of the barn were in much need of repair. It appeared to still be in use. Although no animals inhabited the stalls, there was a great deal of tools lying about. Every inch of space was put to good use. It seemed a good enough place to sleep.

Looking up at the rafters, she came across an old loft. The loft was loaded down with bales of hay. No ladder. A small smile formed on her face. She guessed it would be a problem for any other person. Not for her. Springing into the air with little effort, she landed with very little noise, only the smallest crackling of hay.

She settled into the hay, and her dreams claimed her, as if they had been waiting to be seen. Perhaps they had been waiting, but her life in the city had blocked them out. Too much chaos in her life that even her dreams could not reach her. No rhyme or reason to them. They all wanted to be heard. One insisted on being seen. A lustful image of a man—no, a god with a body made for sin. Her body reacted to his image as if a red-hot iron had burned her bare skin. Her flesh was hot, her body ached with desire. Serena felt his touch on her body in sensitive places. Places that had not been caressed in far too long. His rigid cock pressed hard against her backside, rubbing until it lay between the cleft of her perfectly shaped bottom. He bent her over a long wooden table, toying with her until she begged him to end the torture. Tension formed in her body with each caress she felt. With each thrust and rock of his hips. He knew how to move to drive her crazy and have her begging for more. She awoke on a gasp to an orgasm that rocked her senses, her fangs elongating with her excitement.

Coming out of her dazed, climaxed sleep with a smile on her face, she stretched with the laziness of a tomcat. The haze cleared from her mind as her eyes adjusted to the light. For one brief moment, she was confused as to where she was. She briefly thought the events of yesterday were a dream. It slowly came back to her, noises filtering into her mind. Metal banging against metal, one giving way to the other as the heated material was shaped into something new.

Serena peered over the edge of the loft to see if any soul was about. She had to get outside without being seen. It wouldn't do if she were jailed for trespassing. No telling what they'd do to her. No room for an immortal to make mistakes. Even the slightest error could cost her, her life.

Opening her senses, scanning the barn, making sure nobody's around. Satisfied that the barn was clear, she jumped down, landing with a soft thud. Sound barely heard, if one was paying attention. She looked a sight. Fixing herself the best she could, Serena pulled hay from her hair and gown. Too bad there was no mirror. She really could use one right about now.

Moving closer to the open barn door, she peeked out to see where the sound was coming from. Moving toward the back of the barn, Serena stopped in her tracks when she saw the man working so hard. He must have been in his late sixties, maybe even in his early seventies.

Serena came to her senses and out of shock enough to clear her throat. "Pardon me, sir."

Watching, he put his tools down and turned to her. All the while, she prayed her style of dress did not upset him. While her gown was fashioned to her favorite period, it still revealed much. For now, she knew it was of great importance that she watch him carefully; his first impression of her was very critical. Serena might need an ally, even a minor one. His facial features did not change, but his energy sure did. That told her more than any sign would.

"MiLady, how may I be of service to ye?"

Aware she had to be careful in what she said to this man. His dress and his language told her much. It did not tell her enough. She needed to find out as much as possible. How was she to go about it? She would have to bend the truth a lot. Her stomach turned with the thought of telling a falsehood.

"Forgive me for disturbing ye. I fear I am lost. I have been wandering around for days," she said with a smile meant to melt his heart, being very careful not to show too much of her teeth. "I must confess to ye. I slept in yer barn last night. I do hope ye forgive me."

"MiLady, nay need for forgiveness. I should beg ye forgiveness for the lack of my manners. I am known around these parts as Milton," he said with a very welcoming smile as he bowed.

She could tell it had taken him a great deal of effort. Reaching out to him, she helped him to straighten. "Please do not exert yerself, sir. Ye do not need to bow to me, for we are equals. Would ye be so kind as to show me where I may freshen up?"

The expression on his face spoke of his shock. He was horrified by her suggestion of them being—equals. By his reaction, she imagined her presumption was like saying a four-letter word. Serena was not sure if she should atone for the way she spoke. The choice was simple. No, she would not. She did not want to make herself seem guilty.

Not saying a word, he simply turned and gestured for her to follow him with the wave of his hand. Serena fell into step behind the elderly gentleman. Her soul absorbed the beauty of the landscape and the silence it offered. A welcome change from the entire racket of noise the city provided.

"I take ye to Sir Argyle keep, milady. His home is far more fitted to ye. I have but a small croft. 'Tis nay suitable for a lady," he said with a faint smile.

She turned her head to fully look him in his face, not sure if she wanted to meet this Sir Argyle. The look on his face was a forced one. Perhaps she would wait to meet this man before judging him.

Before she let it rest, one question, what is this man's true nature? "Is he a nice man?"

She was not sure he heard her until she heard the sound, he made low in his throat. A sound he meant her not to hear. He did not comment on her question at once. When he did answer, it was in a roundabout way.

"Who is capable of commenting on a mon's character, lass? Ye may gauge him for yerself."

The tower castle came into view moments later. Standing out against the lush green background, it loomed over the valley, a dark, threatening manor. No hint of light. No pleasure, just shadows, shadows stretching across the vibrant land. The light shied away from the darkness the castle yielded. No comfort or joy radiated from the building. Evil ran deep, deep into the heart of each and every stone that made up this fortress.

Serena followed silently beside the old man as he escorted her to the main gate. Eeriness washed over her. Like an iced blanket wrapped around her bare hot flesh, chilling her to her bones. No good could or would come from this place.

Serena watched the many faces walk by her, pretending not to look her way. Each conveyed a look of hopelessness, desperation deep within their eyes. Every one of them silently warned her to flee while she still could. Perhaps she should listen to the silent pleas.

"Here ye are, milady. Let us make our way to the main door."

"Yes, let us see if any are home."

There was something the old man was not telling her. There was the slightest chance he did not know. Either way, she was about to find out. A voice rang out, and she watched all cease doing their activities as if the smallest of movements would draw attention to themselves. What kind of man was he that his own tenants feared him?

Her eyes roamed across the sea of motionless bodies, settling on a fat, bald, medium-height man. The aura about him spoke of the kind of man he was—evil. It radiated from his every orifice. When he spoke again, it made her skin crawl. She supposed she should speak at the very least explain her situation.

"Excuse me, Sir Argyle. It seems I have misplaced my manners. May I introduce myself? I am Lady Serena Wulff," she said as she flashed him her best smile.

Watching as Sir Argyle slowly let his eyes skim over her body. The smirk that settled on his face was one of approval and deception. She found herself wondering if he knew it. Probably not. He had the look of a man absorbed in himself.

"Lady Serena, nay need for apologies. Many often lose their manners in my presence," he said with the smuggest of looks on his face. As if he meant her to agree with him about his superior look.

Serena found herself unable to agree with him. Instead, nodded her head, as if to agree with him. She'd let him think what he wanted.

As he invited her into his home, the entire time he kept talking about whatever pleased him. His ramblings made her head hurt. She wasn't in any kind of place or situation to comment.

Out of politeness, she would give an, "Oh, yes," or, "I see," when she thought he wanted an answer. Of course, always making sure the response fits.

As he showed her around his home, Serena noticed the slightest touches of a woman, however subtle they were. A compulsion came over her. One so strong that she fought the urge. It was none of her business where his wife was. For all she knew, his wife was dead, and bad memories were better off, buried deep within oneself. Pulled from her thoughts back to her current reality by a question from his lord that she simply couldn't give a short response to.

"I am sorry, Sir Argyle, but I fear I did not hear yer question."

"I understand, from Milton that ye are lost."

"Aye. I was with friends, and somehow, I got separated from them. Ye see, I am not from here; I really don't know my way around yer beautiful country."

She could not tell a falsehood. She never could. She figured a little truth was better than none at all. She had always hated the weaving of truths and lies that came so easily in the modern world. People convincing themselves a little white lie wouldn't hurt the person they were telling it to, never giving it much thought after it was spoken. At this very moment, it was in her best interest to weave in as much of the truth as possible. It would allow her to keep her untruths straight. She was from the future, and she didn't think it wise to state this.

"Ye are more than welcome to stay in my keep until ye find yer way back to yer friends' home."

It was meant to be inviting, yet there was something sinister behind it. It seemed everyone knew it. Including her. Following quietly behind the chambermaid leading her to her room, all the while feeling secrets lingering about. Serena entered a room bigger than the whole of her apartment, thanking the maid for her time.

She turned to go deeper into the chamber, and then she heard the whisper. "Beware."

Strolling around the room, she took in the lavishly decorated chamber inch by inch. Serena hadn't been in a room like this for centuries. However, she still remembered the secrets they held. It did not take her long to find what it hid. The bolthole, is hidden in the far corner behind a changing screen. It appeared Sir Argyle had plans of his own. This was not going to do. She walked over to the fireplace for wood, finding pieces thin enough to wedge into the wall. There would not be any midnight guests in her room—at least, not one that had not been invited.

Chapter Five

Hours had elapsed since she had shimmed the bolthole shut. Pacing the floor, she pulled free the dagger. Would the blade take her back if her blood touched it once again? Was this the answer to her dreams? Would she be able to revert back to what she had once been, to be left alone to be happy? She did not know the answers to these questions. Certain times were one thing she had on her side at the moment, at least until she figured this situation out.

Hunger took over with a need so strong that she could feel her own blood running through her veins. Smelled the other occupants within the keep. Heard their hearts pumping what she so desperately craved. There was nothing close at hand to sustain her hunger, no quick run to her refrigerator. She needed to get out without being seen. The bolthole came to mind. Where did it lead? The window—now, that was something she could use. Leaning out the window and looked down, needing to see what was out there. It was a long way down—about a sixty- to seventy-foot drop. That was nothing for her, nor was it an issue to get back up. She hoped no one would come to her door. To make certain no one entered, she'd bar the door shut.

She headed to the freedom the window offered. Leaping onto the ledge and peering over, making sure all was clear before she committed herself to air. Nobody was in sight as she jumped out and floated down to the earth below. Adjusting her dress, she started out at a fast pace away from the dark shadows. Even as she grew farther from the keep, it seemed the animals stayed far away.

A scent on the winds carried her to a nearby clearing. The tall grass swayed in the winds, sending its fragrances up into the air. Mixed within was the sweet scent of love. She did not want to kill them, but she knew she couldn't let them live. Her hunger was too great, and the mere smell of them caused her heart to beat faster. At least she could make it a quick, painless death.

Their heartbeats pounded in her ears like conga drums beating out a Latin rhythm. A hot, sultry beat that spoke of sexual acts so primitive. An act it's been done since the beginning of time. An act that brought great pleasure, if preformed right. There was no doubt in her mind that this man knew what he was doing. They would have this pleasure one more time.

Serena watched from a distance. Mesmerised by the musk and the sexual energy that radiated through the air. Yet still nearby to see every thrust of this man's well-sculpted backside. Every muscle in his magnificent body flexed with every rock and pull of his hips. His taut, hard, tanned flesh stood out against the creamy-white softness his partner offered. She clung and wrapped herself around him as her climax neared. As their orgasms echoed across the clearing, Serena attacked.

They didn't hear or see her coming. Serena snapped their necks in one swift motion, a blur to the human eye. It happened so quickly that there was no time for them to react. No scream or whimper was made. It was not the way she wanted to feed. She preferred to feed while their heart still pumped.

There had once been a time she would have wined and dined her volunteers. Maybe even glamour them into thinking she loved them. But this would have to do. She stepped out of her gown, knowing full well she would make a mess by taking two lives quickly. No blood could be on her, no evidence.

Their bodies lay limp on the ground, lifeless. Her fangs sank deep into their soft flesh. There already was a difference in the taste and texture of the blood. The warmth of the blood quickly faded, and the bitter cold of the dead set in. Cold only the dead were privy to. It was different from blood chilled in one's fridge. Even now, with the frigidness setting in, the blood was a thousand times purer than a body from her time had tasted. Now was not the time to ponder on the subject. She needed to drink her fill. No matter the eeriness it brought. No time to waste. Feeding until her sides ached and her stomach felt as if it would burst, retracking her fangs and saying a silent prayer for their souls. For there was no telling when she would be able to feed again. Now was definitely the time to indulge oneself in gluttony. The feel of the plasma bursting in her mouth, coating the lining of her oral cavity, was pure heaven.

Feeling full as a kitten stuffed with mother's milk, Serena gazed down at the bodies, realizing she could not leave them out for the elements to deal with. She knew she was hungry. But she did not grasp how crazed she had become as she feasted on their blood. Bite and claw marks everywhere. No inch is left untouched. As the blood seeped slowly from the bodies, it mingled with the earth below. Staining the vibrant green grass crimson. Blood dried on their flesh around the open wounds.

Serena knew there was no way to make it look as if an animal had done this evil act. It was far too evident to her; that a human had caused their death. A silent laugh echoed in her head. She'd watched one too many crime scene shows. And now, they all seemed to reverberate within her mind. She was the newcomer in these parts. Therefore, all eyes would be on her. No turning back from this. What had she done?

She needed to put them underground. But that was not possible. There was not enough time to do so. When it came down to it, there was nothing she could do. Best if she got as far away as possible from the scene of the crime. Serena had to get back to her chamber before someone came looking for her. She did not want to try to explain what she was doing here, as naked as the day she had been born, and with two dead bodies.

She made her way back to the keep. At the same time, she scanned the area around her, making sure nobody was watching. The closer she got, the more people were about. None of them seemed to look around. All kept their eyes on the task at hand. Working out of fear, not out of loyalty to their lord. She reached the wall of the keep, taking one last look around before she committed herself to air. Finding no eyes on her, she floated up to the window ledge. Climbed into her chamber and took a deep breath, relieved by the safety it offered even if it was a false comfort.

Her body demanded to rest. No telling when someone would come looking for her, and she had to be at the top of her game. Serena lay in bed as she awaited the commotion and cries to fill the halls of the keep once the bodies were found. Undoubtedly, she would hear the screams of the villagers once they found their friends. Closing her eyes, she waited in silence for the first bloodcurdling scream.

Time went by, and not a sound was made. What was wrong with these people? Eventually, they were sure to notice two bodies missing. Two strong, young bodies, able to do the hard labour the old were no longer capable of doing. Someone surely would begin to wonder where his or her son or daughter had gone. Wouldn't they? But there was simply nothing, and it had been far too long for them not to have been found.

A sigh escaped her lips as she realised she would have to go down to the great hall to see if anything was amiss. With that thought, a knock came at the door. Opening the door wide, she found the maid who had shown her to her room standing before her.

"I beg ye pardon, milady. Sir Argyle wishes ye to come down to the great hall," she said, trying not to look at her too much.

"I am sorry. I fear I have forgotten yer name."

"Ye wish to know me name, milady," she said in a shocked tone but did not hesitate to give it. "I am Aaid Megan Munro, but me friends call me Meg."

"Well then, Meg, a pleasure to meet ye. Please call me Serena. No need for ye to say milady, not if we're going to be friends," she said, slipping her hand into hers. "Come. Show me where I am needed."

"Milady, I could nay call ye by yer given name," she said, shaking her head so fast that she looked like a hummingbird. "I would be punished severely for such defiance."

Serena saw the fear in her eyes. It was something she knew all too well. She did not wish to put her in any danger.

"Well, I do not wish ye to be hurt. I still would like it if ye called me by my given name." She knew that she understood by the smile she gave her.

They walked in silence, enjoying the companionship of each other. As they walked, she felt the change in Meg as quickly as it happened. Serena waited in silence for her newly found friend to speak her mind on what had her quiet as a church mouse. She did not wait long for her to verbalise what weighed heavily on her mind.

"Milady, oh, forgive me, Serena. 'Tis going to get some getting used to," she said with a sigh. "Ye need to get as far away from here as possible while ye still can. This place and Sir Argyle are pure evil. Something in the land keeps us here, something that holds ye whether ye wish it or not." She stopped, turning to look at her as if she wished to say more.

Before she could ask Meg what was on her mind, she heard the voice of Sir Argyle. Stifling the frustration she felt, she patted Meg on the hand. "Ye may tell me later what else ye fear," she said with a smile.

Entered the great hall with a calm that came all too natural to the predator within, she did not want them to see any kind of weakness within her. Serena knew if weakness was spotted, they'd take full advantage of it. Then, she would be trapped. Compelled to watch all around her until she was able to leave this dark place. She had to find secrets. Secrets hidden so deep, even the holder held the illusion of safety. Power over Sir Argyle would be the instrument to her safety.

Serena scanned the room in one swift motion, taking note of all within the dining hall. Many faces graced the room, and Sir Argyle and his companions didn't seem to take notice. It was in those hidden faces they didn't seem to see which held the secrets. Secrets concealed by layers of pure fear. Private memories she would tap into.

Pulled from her thoughts Serena moved toward Sir Argyle at once as he began to introduce her to his companions. There was something in the way he did it which was hidden beneath the surface. She smiled and nodded to each man as she made her way to her seat, indicated by Sir Argyle. Sitting quietly as servants placed platters of food on the table, watching their faces for any hint that they had found the bodies she had brutally murdered. There was nothing, they were expressionless, no hint that would give her any clue if they knew anything. Serena glanced over to where Sir Argyle and his friends sat, curious as to what they were discussing.

They didn't stop talking as they piled food upon their trencher. As if they feared the food would be taken away at any moment. Serena watched the men as she placed very little upon her trencher, just enough to look as if she was eating. Just enough to help plant the idea firmly in their minds. Serena watched as they ate, the sight of it made her stomach turn and she thanked the heavens, she was not eating. Knowing her stomach would purge its contents at the sight of them. They shovelled food into their mouths, barely giving themselves time to swallow. Hell, forget swallowing. They didn't give themselves time to masticate the food. She watched in disgust as juices from meat squirted and flowed out of their mouths. Serena doubted they knew just how sickly they made her feel. There was no taking the time to wipe their faces for the pretence of good manners. Not once did they attempt to pick up what utensils had been laid out before them. She turned away from the sight as they stuffed their faces with handfuls of berries. There was not one living soul in the room who didn't feel revolted by what was portrayed for all to see.

Serena caught a glimpse of Meg carrying a tray of food up a narrow staircase, hidden behind a tapestry. She made a mental note to check it out later. First, she needed to leave the great hall, so she sought the permission needed.

"Pardon me, Sir Argyle. May I be excused for the eve? I fear I am in need of rest," she said with the slightest bit of tension in her voice.

Gaining her permission, she swiftly left the room.

A sound captured her attention as she made her way to the chamber. Perking up her ears, she turned her head ever so slightly in the direction of the muffled sound. Who or what had made that sorrowful wailing? Night was soon upon them and, with it, a sleeping keep. There would be plenty of time to silently search her surroundings.

Chapter Six

Seumas and William rode side by side without saying a word, an unspoken agreement to remain silent.

"Do ye not wish to know what we seek?" asked Seumas.

"Well, aye, I know what we seek. I do not know where we seek it."

"Let me tell ye where we seek it then. 'Tis alleged to hide in a body of water, water that shimmers silver upon its ripples."

"I would think somebody would have found it by now, milord," said William with a hint of laughter in his voice.

"Aye, ye would think so. Yet it remains hidden from all. The legend says it shows itself to whom it chooses. Nay all sees what the water truly is. To many, 'tis nothing more than water ye drink, bathe, and wash with. 'Tis why the crystal has yet to be found. It shows its precious secret to a chosen few. Once the beholder of the crystal has no need for it or the beholder has passed away, it returns to its water," he said as he studied the ring in his hand.

"My friend, let's us hope it shows its true nature to ye then," said William with laughter vibrating his voice.

"Aye, let's us hope she shows some mercy."

He turned his attention back to the ring on his finger. His uncle had bequeathed it to him, and in doing so, he'd instructed him to keep it near at all times. He now wondered if it would help him to find the crystal. He could think of no other reason his uncle would have made such a remark. Still, it had not helped his uncle in his quest. There had to be more to unlocking the secret to the crystal he so desperately sought. Seumas desired the hopefulness it offered and all the possibilities that came along with it. Now was the time for him and him alone. Time for new beginnings and the peace of mind that came along with it.

The memories of his wife and unborn child no longer haunted him. His time of suffering and torment had ended in one swift vision. A vision that brought forth feelings of assurance, peace, and desire. Seumas's body hummed with the energy those feelings and thoughts brought. That same energy resonated the ring alive, awakening it in a way he had never seen. It glowed with newly found life within him. With each thought he had of a woman he did not know, it seemed to glow even brighter. As if it knew something he did not. Mayhap it did, and that possibility was something he looked forward to.

Nevertheless, for now, he was going to put all his energy, all his effort into finding the sacred waters. He would not be riding away empty-handed. He knew the crystal held great power, and in the wrong hands, it could be dangerous. Power often changed man into great leaders or destructive villains.

He needed to see what his future held for him and all those he loved. To see what was deep inside his heart. Moreover, to help his dear friend with the problem he had, a problem that was not a little matter at all. He knew about the affair he was having. He might not be married, but she was. This was not something he approved of. Nor was it something he could look lightly upon. Before he could broach the subject with his friend, he needed to see what was ahead of William. This was the only way he would be able to help William out of a situation requiring a delicate touch. There was just one catch. He had to find the crystal first.

Two days passed, and still, there was a great distance to cover before they arrived at their destination. Even then, he had to be worthy enough for the waters to show their true colours. To show its silvery shimmer and the secret it held. It would show itself to him. Something changed deep within him. A change even he felt. Every ounce of his body had come alive in days past.

They rode fast and hard in the direction of the loch and his future at hand. It seemed to be what they both needed. The sun was beating down upon him, warming his flesh. Causing his skin to tingle as the cool wind rushed up against his body, trying to push its way through him, only to beat up against a solid wall. The same wind brought the smells of the earth to him. The scent of flowers and heather mingled together in the air with a slight hint of dew. But there was something else on the winds that called to him. An aroma so unfamiliar to him, but a fragrance he recognized all the same. It tugged at his senses, at his very being. He knew it would become clear to him. All he needed to do was wait. Wait for fate to do its work.

Fate. That was something to laugh at. He had found fate to be a fickle wench. Providence had not been kind to him so far. It was fate that had taken all from him. So, why would it be compassionate to him now? Why restore what it had already seen fit to take away? Then again, mayhap it was all part of her plan.

Had it not been said, "What's meant to happen will happen?" He had definitely become stronger with each blow dealt to him. Still, he was uneasy about fate playing in any part of his life. He wanted to have full control of that area, and the crystal could give it to him. William and he had a lot in common when it came to their lives. He would have control of his life and his future at hand.

His attention was brought back at once when he heard William call out. He found himself gazing upon the water that lay out in front of them. The water was close, yet still so far away to see if the water shone silver within its ripples. Seumas spearing his mount to an unholy pace, he raced for watery banks. His hopes ran high with anticipation of their possible find. He felt alive. He heard his blood pounding in his ears. Felt his heart beating in his chest.

Bending forward on his horse, he became one with the beast. As his eyes reached the same level as his hand, he saw it. The ring glowed and flashed in a quick rhythm. A rhythm that was unholy. He had never seen light of its kind in all his years. This had to be a sign of some sort. Had to be the water he sought.

Chapter Seven

Serena waited, perched on the oversized bed in her chamber with the door barred from unwanted intruders of any kind. Yet it was not only the bedroom door she must watch, but the bolthole as well. She was about ready to give up on the idea of Sir Argyle trying to enter her chamber from the secret passage hidden within the room. However, she was not disappointed in her guess of Sir Argyle's plots. Muffled sounds fumbling about in the dark came from behind the thick stone wall. If one listened very closely, you could hear what was said. It was quite apparent to her that this man did not know the meaning of tact.

A smile curved her lips at the hint of amusement she found in the current situation. She could almost see and feel the frustration he was feeling. After a few minutes passed, he gave up, and the noise behind the wall stopped as he went deeper into the passageway. It would be interesting to see what his actions were in the morning. For now, she was going to find out who or what was hidden in the tower.

She could only hope whatever she discovered would help enlighten her about the people she found herself with.

She knew she would need to leave this place as soon as possible. Maybe she would get lucky and find a person jailed in the tower. Before she made choices, she wanted to see what was up there. No use in getting her hopes up for them just to come crashing down.

Serena entered the great hall with utter caution, not wishing to disturb the sleeping servants. As hard as they worked, only the keep's walls coming down around them would wake this group. Pity bubbled to the surface. She quickly banished the feeling. They had been born into this life. More like trapped in this life. Serena shook her head at herself for the thought. They bemoaned their fate. They would rather have a lord they did not fear. A master who saw them and knew them as people. One who understood the plight of their everyday life. The least she could do was not make a sound, let them get their much-needed sleep.

As she approached the stairs, eeriness washed over her, a silent warning to all, a warning that radiated outward from the blackness of the narrow opening. Darkness that sucked in the joy of life and vanquished it until nothing was left but sorrow. The pitch-black stairwell didn't hinder her. Serena definitely could use the darkness to her advantage. Making her way up the narrow stairwell without one sound being made, listening very carefully for even the smallest of noises. Nothing. She found that very odd. Opened her senses to their fullest capacity, trying to find any sign of life behind the thick door. Pausing in her steps, she heard a very dim heartbeat. The door was barred from the outside with a very thick beam. Obviously, someone wanted to keep whomever or whatever in. Serena reached for the handles. She pulled the bolt side and pushed open the door.

Light flowed from the room, caustic to her eyes, and she needed a moment to adjust. She was unable to adapt to the change of light quickly enough, and something hit her. Pain flooded her senses. Enough to rattle her perception. Not giving her assailant another opportunity to attack her, she reached for the heart. Lifting her attacker off the floor. She could feel the struggle under her grasp.

The pain cleared, and her eyes took in images once again. Hissing, she looked at the squirming body in her hand. Her eyes locked with a terrified blue-eyed woman. Yet she was not going to ease up on her hold until she was sure there would be no further attacks. Serena lowered the woman until her feet touched the ground, but still kept hold of her, not yet willing to trust the woman in her grasp.

A sudden realisation struck. Even though she set her back on her feet, there was still fear in the woman's eyes. It did not hit her until she heard the very soft whisper. "What are ye?" she asked with a tremble in her voice.

Oh, dear God, she was baring her fangs. Letting go of her captive with a curse upon her lips, Serena turned, not wishing to face the beautiful lady in front of her. It took a minute to get her feelings and fears under control. Once she felt relaxed, she turned, fangs pulled back in.

Stepping forward to try to comfort the blue-eyed beauty with the utmost serene expression, Serena did not take offence to the terror in her eyes or the fact that she had backed away from her. Instead, Serena searched her mind for the right words to say in hopes of calming the terrified woman before her.

"I'm truly sorry for frightening ye. As well as if I have harmed ye in any way," Serena said with a calmness she did not feel.

Serena knew if she could not get her to understand or believe she was safe, then there was a great chance she would tell her secret to all. She would have no choice but to kill her. Taking a deep breath to soothe her nerves, she started once again.

"My name is Serena Wulff. By what name may I call ye?" she asked in a very sweet tone. As she waited for her to respond, Serena scanned the room she now found herself in.

"I… I am Lady Kari Argyle. I am Sir Argyle's wife," she said in a very bitter tone. She looked at Serena with a caution born of great fear. "Did my husband send ye to kill me?" she asked without hesitation. " 'Twould not be the first time he tried," she murmured as she turned her back to Serena. "I do not wish to see it coming. If ye'd please get it over with," she said as she held her breath.

"I do not wish to kill or harm ye, Lady Kari. I but wish for yer assistance."

"Assistance! How do ye wish I help ye? I can nay even aid meself," she sighed. "I have been a prisoner of my husband since the day of my wedding night. I just did not know it. This tower has been my prison from that day to this."

"Why have ye not tried to escape from this place?"

"At first, I did not because I feared death. When I finally gathered the courage to do so, I was told of my kinsmen's slaughter. Nowhere for me to run to for safety, so I lived with my fortune. The first few years were the hardest. All else 'twas easy."

It seemed once she started recounting her tale, it poured out of her.

"I dealt with my fate, and I slowly started to win the hearts of a few brave souls. The ones I befriended showed me the hidden passages out of the keep." She turned and looked at Serena. She saw the hope in Serena's eyes and quickly banished it. "Do not get yer hopes up, milady. Ye might escape for a brief respite, but this place draws ye back. 'Tis a draw most cannot ignore, nay matter how hard ye try. Most all have tried and failed. I have lived for the brief moments of happiness I have found."

"Does Sir Argyle not ask for ye? Is this why ye take the chance of freedom?"

"Nay, my husband does nay seek me any more. If he does, he's told I have taken ill, and he asks nay further." Turning back to face her, she gave Serena the once-over.

Whatever she searched for, she found. Though there was the slightest of hesitation easily seen within her, still, she spoke. "I do wish I were able to aid ye to flee this dark place. I fear I would feel the draw too greatly. The more times I leave the holding the faster and harder it comes. This land 'tis bewitched, 'tis the only explanation. I have seen many try to escape. All end up back here. So, ye see, truly nay hope," she said with a sigh.

Serena moved backwards toward the corner of the room. Serena recalled the warnings silently sent her way with each glance and look she was given. No need to escape. She had a way out. The story she had told to Sir Argyle. Would he let her walk away? The answer, she knew, would be a resounding no. Hell, the man had already tried to get into her room. What, did he plan to use her as he pleased, then dispose of her? She wouldn't put it past him.

"Are ye willing to leave if I went with you?" she said, feeling compelled to ask. She had a suspicion, deep within her, that all it would take for Kari to be set free was strong willpower. Only there lay the problem. Lady Kari was precisely that—a lady. A very meek, subservient well-born female, her will as easily bent as a blade of grass. Serena returned her gaze back to those blue eyes that could hypnotise a body into surrendering all. At that moment, she knew there was more than hope. They had a good fighting chance of leaving this cursed piece of land.

Someone's coming! They did not try to hide the fact that they were. Looking back at Lady Kari, she gave her a silent warning. Lady Kari's nod of her head was enough of an acknowledgment that she understood what was being conveyed to her.

"I can assist ye. Let me put a stop to this here and now."

"Nay, he mustn't know ye know about me," Kari said as she glanced over to the door. "Nay matter what ye see, ye can nay help."

The rumbling of the voice echoed in the room as if the shouting was happening in the room itself. That was when it hit her. The door was not barred. Serena moved into the darkness of the corner as the door thrust open. The heavy oak and iron door smashed against the stone wall, sending bits and pieces of wood flying through the air.

Serena watched from the concealed corner of the room. The scene played out before her. She watched as the colour in Lady Kari's face drained out. A look of horror replaced the calm, serene expression in her eyes. She knew fear when she saw it, and it was staring her right in the face. With a look she was all too familiar with, Lady Kari locked gazes with her. Yet a moment before she could offer help, Lady Kari hit the floor. Shock swept over her as she watched the incident before her.

Serena flinched as each large bloody fist pummeled the soft-bodied women below them. Blood dripping from Sir Argyle's fists splattered as it hit the floor beneath him. A fine mist of blood sprayed the surrounding area. There was no care taken not to make a mess. She felt her pulse quicken as her fangs pushed out of her tissue when the aroma hit the air.

Lady Kari was thrown around as if she were nothing more than a rag doll. She fought against the urge to attack, against the need to sink her fangs into his flesh and drain him dry. Instead, she hid in the shadows, witnessing the bloodbath before her. Serena shook her head at her own thoughts about *CSI: Crime Scene Investigation* and how they would have handled this case. She could see Grissom and his team working at this crime scene. Reality knocked her back to her senses as she was pinned between the wall and a very limp body. Then, the heavy door slammed shut once again.

Serena reached around the limp body as she searched for a pulse on her slim neck. It took a minute to find one, but when she did, it was strong. Thank the heavens for that. Moving out from underneath the limp body Serena searched for a first aid kit of any kind. Whatever that might consist of. No need to look very hard. She found it all in a small wooden box beside the bed. She wondered how often these beatings took place to have such a well-stocked medical kit. Someone here must care for her. That would be the only reason for the kit to be kept fully stocked.

It took very little doing, but she managed to move the limp form onto the soft bed without doing any more injury. Cleaning the blood took a great deal of her energy, not to bite into the soft, warm flesh. There were few cuts upon her. The ones she did sustain were deep. She needed her rest. Nothing else could be done. With a sigh of regret, she turned to the door, ready to leave.

"Oh shit, the door!" She had not even thought about the door.

To her surprise, it wasn't barred.

As she made her way back to her chamber, Serena sent up a silent prayer. She would leave, and so would Lady Kari. Moreover, anyone else who wished to depart this dark place and their sleazebag master would be leaving with them. Sir Argyle made douchebags look like angels compared to him.

Chapter Eight

All within Seumas came to life at that very moment. The ring on his finger was desperate to leap off his hand. As he ran his hand through the water to feel the coolness it offered. 'Twas more than that. He wanted to see the silver shimmer upon his flesh. The contact with the water cooled his heated skin. Taking a few steps back, he was unable to truly believe he had found the sacred water. The same light he saw in his ring shot out of the water. Flooding the space between him. He closed his eyes and thanked the gods for allowing him to find it.

" 'Tis what ye seek, milord?" asked William.

"Aye. Ye nay see the shimmer upon the water?"

"Nay, can nay 'Tis clear water. 'Tis, as ye say though, not all see the water for what it truly is."

"Aye, must be the case. I had hoped ye would be able to see it. 'Tis a glorious sight to see."

"Truly filled with delight for ye, milord. Ye found what ye sought. I hope it brings ye the peace ye seek."

"Thank ye, my friend. I wish for the same. Let us rest for a while. 'Tis been a long day of riding, and night's now upon us."

"'Mayhap eats some of those nice sandwiches cook was so nice to make."

"Aye, let us refresh ourselves with a short respite. Seems I've ignored my body's needs. For now, my stomach pains me with the mere thought of food."

"Think the water safe for our mounts?" William asked as he fetched the food and wine from the packs.

"The water's fine. The horses won't be harmed," said Seumas with a smile he did not try to hide. He had so much to be thankful for.

Lying on the bank of the loch, he looked up at the starlit sky. There was a mystery within the stars. He had gazed upon them many a night and found shapes by the plenty. This night was nay different, except the patrons kept lining up to form the woman he had seen. A woman he desired to touch and take in her scent. Time was all that was needed.

Time, he thought to himself with a hint of a smile. He would get the crystal and bring peace to his life—or at least to his heart.

Sitting up at once as William approached with their food in hand. Seumas ate with relish as he listened to his friend's tale.

As William was about to reach the punch line, he became very serious in his tone and manner. "Seumas, may I talk to ye? 'Tis consuming my soul," he said with a touch of pain.

He knew it was of importance by the tone in his voice, also by how tense his body became. "Talk to me about whatever ye wish," he said, smiling, trying to ease William's nerves.

"There's a special lass I wish to spend the rest of me life with," he said with a sigh. "Yet I cannot, and 'tis something I can nay change."

"Is it the blunt truth that the lass already has a husband?" he asked without malice. He watched as William's face changed to one of horror. He continued before William could get worked up, "Do not worry yourself, William. I do not think anyone else knows. I was not sure of it myself until this very moment." He turned to fully face William to see what he was feeling before he spoke once more. Satisfied with what he saw in his friend's eyes, only then did he speak. "I won't tell ye what to do. 'Tis wrong, and I know ye know this. It can nay go any further. She is a married lass, which means she has a lawful husband. She might nay love or even like her husband. The plain fact is that she has one. Ye know the law and what the law states. She must be widowed for one season before another may make an offer for her hand."

With that said, he met his friend's gaze. He saw the silent war going on in his eyes. Truth, love, and righteousness battled over one another for control of the man's heart. Seumas saw it, even before William felt it. Righteousness won the fight. It filled his eyes. He knew in an instant that there was no need to say more. Silently, he waited for his friend to speak.

"I did not know what I wanted ye to say until this very moment. A part of me wanted nothing more than for ye to say ye understood. Even a smaller part of me wanted ye to say I could have her despite the fact of her husband. She does nay love him. I knew from the first moment I saw her that she was meant for me. I get to hold her on a rare occasion," he said with a sigh. "Only when 'tis safe for her to escape her prison. Only then does she come to me. First we met, 'twas by chance. She was nay looking for someone. All she wanted was freedom from her gilded prison, however short-lived it might be."

Before he could speak further, Seumas stopped him. "What do ye mean by her gilded prison? Is the lass nay free to come and go as she sees fit?" he asked with an edge to his voice.

Seumas was not sure he liked the sound of a woman kept prisoner in her own keep. Seumas continued to listen to his friend, and he got enraged over what he heard. He did not wish to hear any more.

"Enough," he said as he raised his hand. "Me ears are full. I don't wish to hear any more." Turning to William, he spoke, "I shall think on this to see if I can find a way out for yer woman friend." Seumas knew she was more than a friend, but he did not wish to comment any further on it.

Frustration set in so rapidly that he found himself throwing aside what was left of his food. Aggravated with the fact, he found it impossible to keep his eyes from wandering over to the silvery water. He gave in to the need his body yearned for. Striding over to the water, he stripped off the articles of his clothing, tossing them aside with disregard. There was no stopping at the banks of the water. He simply walked on in, not even flinching at the bitter cold of the freezing water.

The ring came alive on his hand the very moment his body was submerged in the water. It vibrated and hummed on his finger with each pass of his hand through the water. Light shot out from beneath the pond's muddy floor. The same light he had seen from his ring the moment he dove into the cool water. He pulled his way through the water on a very shallow breath. The water kept getting deeper with each pull of his arms. He knew he needed air. He felt his body straining, felt his lungs burn as they were deprived of oxygen. Seumas fought his way back up to the surface of the water for the much-needed air his lungs required. Breaking through the water's glassy surface with a gasp, taking in the much-needed air before he blacked out from lack of air.

Running his hand through his hair, pulling it free from his face, he looked down into the water. He took several deep breaths, stretching his lungs to their fullest capacity, and dived in once more. He went deeper into the water than he had ever thought he was capable of. Lights flashed from the water around him and the ring on his hand. Bubbles floated up from the pond's bed. He must be losing his mind. Searching the muddy earth beneath his hands, he knew in a moment when he had it. He did not need to see it to recognize what he held in his hand. The instant he closed his hand around the crystal, images flooded his mind.

Thoughts he did not dare tell a soul, ones only he understood. He knew they'd be seen as a sign of weakness.

For the first time in a long time, he saw his dead wife and unborn child. They seemed to be saying good-bye. He'd forgotten how beautiful she was. Yet it was not her that made his heart tighten with sorrow. 'Twas seeing his son for the first time. At least what would've been his son, if given the chance to be birthed into the world. He pushed up from the watery depth and came to the surface a second later.

Throwing his tartan across his body, nay caring if he was properly covered from any prying eyes that may be lurking about. Staring at the crystal, he walked over to the tree. What the crystal showed amazed him. He desired to see more.

First, he needed to dry off and quickly rubbed himself dry with his tartan. Seumas arranged his plaid around his waist, making sure each pleat was perfectly in place. Once satisfied, he fastened his belt.

Resting against the moss-padded tree, he took a closer look at the crystal. Upon examination, he found a piece of it missing. He looked at the ring in his hand. The shape of the stone looked as if it would fit perfectly. Seumas needed a second pair of eyes—William. He had almost forgotten all about William. He could tell William was lost in thought, but he needed his help.

"William, can ye come over here for a moment?"

He watched as his friend walked over and knew he could now truly help him. There was a considerable need for him to put his friend's mind and heart at ease. He would—and soon.

Chapter Nine

Serena changed her mind as she headed back to her chamber. "Screw this shit," she said out loud for all to hear. "I'm going to look around Argyle's study." Maybe she would find something that explained why all stayed or why, once they left this dark place, they came back.

She had to find his office. It did not take her long, and she knew it in a moment—the only door locked. Pulling her hairpins free from her hair knowing, they would make quick work of the lock. Serena knelt down in front of the door to get a better look at the lock. Simply made. Not much thought went behind it. Slipping the pins into the keyhole, she felt around for the notches. Feeling as each pin fell into place, quickly turned each one to release the latch. A soft click, and with that, the door came open. Pushing the door wide, she walked in, then silently closed the door behind her. Not wanting to let anyone on to what she was doing.

The room was well furnished. A vibrant, thick plush rug covered the dark wood floor. An ornately carved desk, stained in a dark finish and polished until it shone, sat upon the rug, accompanied by an oversized leather chair. A closer look at the desk revealed Celtic knot work that had been painstakingly worked into the wood. Adjacent to the desk sat two wooden carved armchairs that complemented the desk. Silk tapestry covered the walls, displaying a picture of a proud, handsome man with a falcon on his arm. She could only guess it was a likeness of Sir Argyle. Serena could not help but laugh, for there was no likeness to it. She knew it was how he saw himself and not as the fat, balding man he truly was. Maybe this likeness was he as a young lad and not what he had become.

Returning her gaze back to the rest of the room, she found more luxuries in one chamber than the whole of the keep. Leather-bound books and scrolls filled the shelves of the wall opposite the door. Turning to see what the last wall held behind her, she found herself gawking at a large fireplace she could stand in and still not touch the top with her head.

Enough of this lollygagging around. Time to get down to business. No better place to start her snooping than with the scrolls. The first couple of parchments were nothing more than tenant arrangements. A medieval rental agreement, if you would. As well as several livestock papers, deeds, and titles to land.

It was getting late, and the day was dawning. She was about to abandon the search when she came across a hidden compartment. It wasn't very big. Big enough to hold one scroll, and it looked to be very old. However, how old was it? Only one way to find out. Retrieving it from its hiding spot, she gently unrolled it on the desk. Glancing at the document, she saw symbols and words she recognized.

Symbols she had not seen in a very long time. Serena took a closer look at the document to read what was written on it. A gasp left her lips as she recognized a binding spell when she read one.

Strong magic was at work here. Sir Argyle required something personal of the person he meant to bind. *Hell bells* – she thought to herself. These people did not have a chance, by the way the document read distant ancestors could very well cursed their family line to servitude by agreeing. This room should be overflowing with the possessions of others. Yet it was not. What else could he have used to cast a spell over so many? A great deal of these people had very little. All they really had to give of themselves that would mean anything to them was their word. Could you bind someone to you by their word and nothing more given? That had to be it. As for Lady Kari, she had bound herself to her husband the day she married him. Nothing more virtuous and purer could be given than oneself. Her purity and innocence had sealed her fate. A fate sealed in blood.

Serena knew of only one way to break free of a spell, and that was with the same magic that had formed it. Well, that was not the only way. The person who was bound by the spell could break free of the curse if they truly wished. They had to be stronger than it. There lay the problem. Most of these people were very weak-minded. She knew she would have to convince Lady Kari to leave with her— the sooner, the better.

Putting back the scroll where she had found it, she backed out of the room. With one last look around the room, she needed to make sure all was in its place. Not wanting to alert anyone of her presence within the chamber.

Glancing out into the corridor she made sure the coast was clear. Satisfied none were around, she left the room. A smile of satisfaction on her face, she heard the latch fall into place.

Serena paused at her chamber door as she listened for the slightest of sounds, someone was in her room. Backing away from the door to get a better look at the edges of the doorframe for any sign of light seeping through, she did not really expect to find the light. She was not disappointed. All the same, someone was in her room. Pushing the door open slowly as she made her way inside, praying it did not make a sound. To her delight, her prayer was answered. The door closed behind her just as quietly. She took in a breath.

The room was pitch-black and still in her unfamiliar surroundings, Serena pinpointed where the person stood. The heartbeat was like a beacon burning bright as the sound of the blood rushed back to the heart. A vascular chart lighting up those sensitive areas, where the blood flowed strong. Serena walked in the direction of the pulsing, not once making a sound, so as not to be heard. Nearing the warmth, she recognized the scent. Lady Kari was in her chamber. With that knowledge, she turned and headed back over to the fireplace. Within mere seconds, a fire was lit and warming the room.

Facing the fire, she addressed her guest. "Lady Kari, how may I help ye?" she asked in a tone that held no surprise at the woman's presence.

No response. Silence. She sought out her face but was only able to see the tips of her slippers.

"Are ye all right?" Serena watched as Lady Kari moved away from the dark shadows the room offered.

Serena knew the pain she must be in; she was limping far too much not to be. Oh God… the swelling and the bruises gracing her face. Serena wished for modern conveniences, like the wonders of ice, at this very moment. If only for her ladyship's battered face, her jaw had to be broken, ice would help ease the swelling. Serena knew there was no way for her to truly know without a radiograph. For someone who wanted nothing more to do with modern laws and way of life, she sure was wishing for its medical care.

Serena was now limited on the assistance she'd be able to offer her ladyship. Only one way for her to check if her mandible was broken, and it would bring a world of pain. What she would give for morphine or Darvocet right about now. She had to examine her, but at the same time, not show too much knowledge.

"Milady, may I inspect yer injuries?" asked Serena with a calmness she did not feel.

A quick hummingbird nod of her head gave consent to the examination. Either she could not verbally speak or speaking caused her a great deal of discomfort. Whichever it was, she understood.

Essentially, she washed her hands before the exam. To her delight, a washstand was near her soon-to-be patient. Pouring the water in the basin enough to wet her hands. Lathering her hands with the nearby bar of soap, making sure to scrape under her nails before rinsing them clean. Satisfied her hands were hygienic enough to examine the mouth and jaw of her ladyship, not wanting to spawn an infection in her already weakened state. Pausing, she reached out to touch the bruised and inflamed flesh long enough to take in a deep breath to steady herself.

"Brace yourself, milady. This might cause ye a great deal of pain. I apologise now for any discomfort," muttered Serena. With that said, she pushed forward with the examination.

Palpation of her facial structure revealed soft, depressible areas in the skeletal bones. Serena had no doubt there were fractures in the maxilla and zygomatic bones. To her astonishment, Lady Kari's nasal bones felt intact. The knowledge of both these areas did very little to make her feel at ease, for she still needed to check the lower jawbone. To her amazement, the mandible was not broken, but dislocated. Knowing what she had to do did not put her at ease. A brief moment of thought warning Lady Kari crossed her mind, Serena knew how much pain she was about to inflect. That was all it was, and this was how she wished it to stay.

To Serena's shock, she did not make a sound. The proof of her agony was evident upon her battered cheeks. She wished she could have saved her from the pain. But what she could do was far more important to her ladyship. She was going to give her freedom from a life of solitude and misery. Solitude and misery were both things Serena was very familiar with. Each accompanied her for far too long, and she longed to be rid of them both. Now was the time for happiness and love to rule in both of their lives. Most of all, freedom from her ladyship's dark imprisonment.

"Ye won't be able to speak for a while without causing yerself pain. I would like ye to nod yer understanding." Serena waited for a response from her ladyship. When she nodded at once, Serena continued to talk, "Do these beatings happen often?"

She watched as she nodded. Anger set in swiftly. "Does it occur whenever he does not get what he wants?"

The nod she knew was coming came. At that moment, Serena knew it was her fault. She had denied him entrance, and in doing so, she'd sent him off in a maddened rage.

"I have one more question for you, milady. Are ye ready to leave this place forever?" Happy to see her eyes light up, she nodded her answer. " 'Tis settled then. When I leave this cursed place, so do ye. Ye need to get yerself back to yer chamber. We don't want him to find ye here with me."

Serena found herself wondering how Kari had stayed alive for so long. Even now, bruised and beaten, there was still a grace about her, strength deep within her. How deep was this strength hidden? Serena knew she would have to help her find it if she was to break the binding spell upon her.

She wanted to give her ladyship time to heal from the trauma her body had received that night. At the same time, she knew she had to make the move while Lady Kari's willpower was still strong. She was going to need all the help she could get. Tomorrow, they would walk right out the front door. Serena knew well there would be a fight. She would be quite disappointed if there was not. An ache lay deep within her, and she wanted to itch it—soon enough.

Chapter Ten

Lady Kari fought for control over her pain and discomfort throughout the night. Her thoughts turned to the prospect of being free of her BASTARD husband. She prayed Lady Serena could deliver what she had offered. Deep down, she knew she could. Her pain dulled to a bearable state as she slipped deep into sleep's warm embrace.

I flew above lush green fields, feeling the freedom the wind offered. Looking down at the land below, I knew this area, and my heart skipped with joy.

William, *my sleeping mind purred.*

I felt him, yet couldn't see him. I landed with a soft thud in hopes of finding my lover. His presence was everywhere. God... if I could only rub my hands and body against his. With that thought, the sky above me darkened, and lightning lit up the now-blackened sky. My name echoed on the winds in an icy-cold voice, cutting through me like a blade. Then, the ground vanished beneath my very feet, and I was falling fast.

Why did she keep hearing her name being called? Someone wanted her, and a warning went off in her head. Roughness in the voice and touch, but underneath it all, there was a demand in the tone. No love in the way her name was said. Kari tried to move, tried to get away from the roughness that was upon her body, there was nay escaping the feeling. Consent pressure against her skin, followed by pain and dampness.

Kari awoke to find herself under knifepoint. To her shock and amazement, she was not frightened. She was not surprised to find her husband held a knife in his hand and its point was held against the soft flesh of her throat. She scrambled back on the bed to get away from Sir Argyle's reach. Once, there was a time she would have jumped onto the blade, ending her torment. This was not one of those moments. Soon, she would have her freedom, and the blade in his hand would not take that from her.

Staring up at her husband, she came to the realisation that he was no longer holding the knife to her. He had gone off on a ranting fit about women. His raving continued out of control, utterly unchecked. His face was a bright crimson, making the whites of his eyes stand out. With each word spat out of his mouth, spit and bubbles accompanied them. That wasn't what grabbed her attention. The vein in the middle of his forehead now protruded and pulsated faster and faster. Looking like it would burst open at any minute. She found amusement in that split second. Almost envisioning steam coming out of his ears. His head burst into flames moments before it popped.

Biting her tongue to stop the laughter from escaping, she did not want to enrage him any further than he already was. Her body was unable to handle another severe beating this soon. Even the lightest touch to her face caused her to wince in pain. No mirror was required to know her so-called beloved husband had badly beaten her. Time would heal her injuries. This time was different. She'd been granted the time to recover from her beating, thanks to her new ally.

Her ears rang as her husband's yelling grew louder. The high pitch of his vibrant yells echoed off the walls of her compact chamber. She watched as he stormed toward the door.

He turned to her with a look in his eyes, hinting at his hatred toward her.

"Ye will not accept visitors until ye are healed. Do we understand one another?"

Did he honestly believe she was actually capable of talking? Could the man nay see how badly beaten her face was? She gave a quick nod of her head, needing to make certain that she understood his request. She wanted to laugh, to scream at the notion of visitors. She was his captive, not his wife or even his lover. Both of those would have the freedom to do as they pleased. She had stopped being his wife the moment she refused his command to be free of her body to his friends. Then, the beatings started and hadn't stopped.

Watching him depart her chamber, she heard herself take in a breath. Not realising she held her breath stunned her. This was her last night. The last time her husband shall ever scare her. For the first time in a very long time, she found herself full of hope and eagerness for the day to start.

Serena stood at the window, gazing out over the countryside. Her eyes settled on the area where she killed and fed.

The image of the two bodies coupling, searching for their release, plagued her mind. Still able to hear their panting as their climax drew near. The aroma of sweat mingling together, oh… God, and the sweet smell of their moist, heated caress. Stirred visions of the man she'd seen back on Mt. Charleston. The sensation he stirred deep within her made her entire body ache with sexual hunger.

She yearned to feel his hands running over her body. Feel the sensation of his lips pressed against her sensitive skin. To have his tongue licking his way down her body, whipping her senses into a frenzy. Serena closed her eyes as her imagination ran wild. Serena felt her body growing taut. Begging for release and it would have it.

Quickly undoing the silk laces holding her dress up, she moved to the bed. Her dress slipped from her body and pooled at her feet. Pausing for the briefest of moments to remove her lacy bra and panties. She didn't need a mortal or immortal man to pleasure her, although she would love to have the service of her vibrator.

Softly caressing her stomach, thighs, working her senses to a heightened peak, she pictured her mystery man. The ache she felt intensified. The mere thought of this man caused her body to react in a way it had not in a very long time. Serena felt her eyes dilate with each image of him. Slowly slipping one hand down her body to softly stroke her heated folds sent a shudder through her. Her movements became demanding. Restless. Fingers stroked in search of her elusive G-spot. She could almost feel him gliding in and out of her sleek, heated warmth. Slamming into her hot, wet mound and grinding on her clit with each powerful thrust of his hips.

"Oh… God. Oh… God, there's the spot," she panted aloud.

Her movements became frantic in her need. Going deeper and harder, pushing against that most sensitive of spots. Her nipples throbbed as her body got near its climax.

She reached for her aching nipples, rubbing, and squeezing them to ease the ache. The sensitive sensation sent her into a powerful orgasm. Serena's body trembled as each wave swept through her.

Lying on the bed, her body gave way to the relaxation it felt. She thought about the pond she had found days ago, its calm silvery water and the coldness it offered. Serena would like to be at the pond right about now. At least she would not find herself in the predicament she was in currently. There would be no saving of genteel ladies. Would not find herself taking two lives in broad daylight. Let alone planning an escape with Sir Argyle's wife. What in the hell was she thinking? There would be no walking out of the keep—at least, not without a fight. Maybe that was what she wanted—a chance to give Sir Argyle a beating he would never forget.

Dawn came quickly. Serena found herself up before the sun even kissed the sky. She sat perched on the arm of a chair, waiting for the sounds of people. Waiting for the sounds of screams. For muffled whispers. Still, there was nothing concerning the two lost souls. The knowledge she would soon be leaving this place eased her mind. This place was wrong, and it was time to leave this dark keep.

Serena headed to Lady Kari's room in a blur of light, essential nobody saw her. The element of surprise was going to be on her side. Serena was delighted to see her ladyship up and ready to go. Glancing around, she noticed there were no bags, not even a small pack. Serena understood this—leaving the old life behind. She had done the exact same thing, giving up the old ways for the new.

Serena explained as quickly and efficiently as possible for her Ladyship. Making sure she understood what was expected of her.

"Ye are to stay behind me or beside me at all times. If it comes to a fight, stay close, but not too close, for I will need space to move. Do not worry about me. I can take care of myself. We need to move as swiftly as possible to make it out of the keep." She did not feel it necessary to inform Lady Kari she had no wish to leave swiftly as possible. The memory of Sir Argyle pummeling his own wife was still fresh in her mind.

Pulled out of her thoughts by Lady Kari's gentle touch.

"Time to go." Grabbing her by the hand, she headed for the door.

Making their way quietly down the stairs as feasibly possible without alerting anyone. Pausing at the bottom of the staircase, pressing her body against the wall as she peered around the corner. The hall buzzed with activity, as she had hoped it would be. She wanted witnesses to what was about to happen.

Taking a deep breath, she turned to her new companion. "Are ye ready for this?"

Not waiting for an answer, she stepped out into the great hall with Lady Kari in tow. It got the response she had intended. All stopped what they were doing. Much to her disappointment, Sir Argyle was not in sight.

"Well, maybe we shall get out of here without yer husband seeing."

Before she knew what was happening, Lady Kari was on the floor, bleeding yet again, Serena saw red. She felt her pupils dilate at the mere smell of fresh blood. She didn't turn to check on her new friend, for there was no time. The next moment, her husband came charging at her, giving little notice to all around him. Serena saw the clenched fist at his side, one dripping with blood. Her own blood boiled in her veins. She never understood the beating of women and children. Serena was happy they did not have children, for that was an innocent that would've suffered in his care. Reacting on instincts, she was in front of Lady Kari's lax form. From this position, she could see the hate running deep within him.

"I suggest, Sir Argyle, ye back away from yer lady wife," she said in a very sharp tone.

Smiling as the mere sound of her voice stopped him dead in his tracks. Causing him to gaze fully upon her, rather than his wife. Putting the full force of his hatred toward her. This irritated her even more so. He had no good excuse for his anger, no reason. He was not the one sprawled out on the cold stone floor, bleeding from his nose.

" 'Tis nay yer affair, Lady Serena. Stand aside."

"I think not."

"Move aside, bitch, or I will have ye moved."

"I see. Either I move of my own accord or ye will have one of yer henchmen do it. Are ye not man enough to do the chore yerself?" she said in a very sweet tone. Happy to see it caused the sting she had intended it to. She knew she had baited him, taunting him openly in front of all in his servitude. He would advance on her. Only to come face-to-face with his mistake, for he only saw her as a weak-minded female.

"Ye try me sorely, woman. Now, move aside," he said as he slowly advanced toward her.

"Well then, ye snake of a man, come and see if I am an easy target, like yer wife," Serena said as she settled into a fighting stance in a silent challenge. Serena glanced over her shoulder to see how her friend fared, she was relieved to see her on her feet with the help of Meg.

Her attention was brought back to the fat, balding man charging her as he howled his fury. She found humour in the way he looked, like a small dog growling and snapping at one's ankles. Alas, she did not have a newspaper to roll up to strike him on the nose to say, *Bad, dog. Bad*. But striking him on the nose would not release her frustration. Serena wanted to hurt him. To make him feel as much pain as his wife had had to endure.

She sprang to life as his first blow came within inches of her face, but he was quick to correct with his left hand. It rattled her teeth a bit, but that was all.

My turn, she thought.

Grabbing hold of his right arm, she twisted it behind his back, pushing up hard as she held him in place. His agonising screams of pain ripped from deep within him. Trying to escape the pain, he leaned forward in a vain attempt to ease the pressure. Adjusting her hold, she bent to his ear.

"I am not as easy to beat, sir," she whispered as she let go of him.

"Ye will regret this, ye stupid bitch," he spat as he rubbed his arm to ease the pain.

"We shall see who regrets this day, sir. Bring yer worst. I do not plan on falling," she said with a hint of malice in her tone.

She knew he had to put a stop to this taunting. For all those around were watching. Intrigued by a face-off by such an ill-matched pair. He needed to keep his authority intact, and she was definitely challenging that authority.

She watched in amusement, as he singled to his men with a slight nod of his head toward her, like she did not notice his movement. Straightening in her stance, she took a breath. She could find these men in a rainstorm. The stench would take weeks of scrubbing to remove the smell from their hides.

Striking her from both sides as they snarled and foamed at the mouth like hungry wolfhounds. Eyes glazed over with a vacant stare. Bodies taut with eagerness for first blood. Each eager to please their master. Unfortunately for them, today would not be such a day. She pitied them. She dispatched them quickly with a snap of their necks. Their bodies dropped like a sack of potatoes hitting the hard floor.

Turning back to square off with Sir Argyle once again. A smile upon her face, only this time, there was no hiding of her fangs. She wished all could see the fear now apparent within his eyes. The fear and trepidation emitting from the very core of him. He knew the end was near. That thought only broadened her smile. This time, there'd be no quick kill. No mercy. He was a predator, one feeding on the weakness of others. Only this time, he came up against one of nature's most feared natural predators.

Chapter Eleven

The first time in too long, Seumas found himself riding off to do the honourable thing—nay, the right thing. His integrity was not in question, just righteousness. After all, William had told him of his lady friend, he found himself using the crystal. What it showed was all he needed to know. 'Tis time someone cared for his friend, time for him to wed a lass. Why not this lass?

Riding through the night toward Lady Kari's lands, they reached the border, and the look in William's eyes said it all. At that moment, he knew he'd made the right decision. William lit up in a way he had never seen before. This was a part of his friend only shown to his lover.

A sense of urgency washed over him as they reached the lower bailey. Something wasn't right. He could feel it. Seumas urged his mount to a faster pace, getting an inkling that whatever was wrong was dire. The gate was wide open, as it should be for this time of the morning, yet where were the guards? Entering the court area revealed how much was truly amiss. The courtyard was empty of its inhabitants. At this hour of the day, there should have been people about, performing the much-needed tasks for the day ahead of them.

They heard the commotion coming from within the dark fortress. Dismounting as quickly and quietly as possible, not wanting to draw attention. Nearing the keep doors, they paused outside, taking in all the sounds and the number of people that might be within. A fight was taking place within. Time for them to show themselves. Their bodies filled the doorway, blocking out the daylight cascading through.

Seumas couldn't believe what he was seeing. Here she was, the woman he had been dreaming about these last few days and nights. She was remarkable, and here she stood, facing off with men much larger than her. By the looks of it, they were in the middle of it. Two men attacked. He moved to intervene but stopped in a few steps. He watched as she dispatched them with great ease, snapping both of their necks. She now squared off with what looked to be their leader. William came up beside him to witness the fight.

" 'Tis Sir Argyle, William?" he inquired, not turning from the fight.

"Aye, 'tis he. Over there stands Lady Kari." William fought against the strong urge to run over to his woman and pull her into his arms.

"Are we to stand here, watching then?" he asked, anger in his voice.

"I am thinking of a way to help. I do not wish to get in the way and bring 'Bout the death of this woman. I fear we're going to have to bide our time for an opening. She might start to weaken."

They closed their distance on the battle at hand. Now hearing every word said. She was taunting him. Leaning in close to whisper something only he could hear. By the looks of it, it caused him to pale.

Serena was ready for a fight, her body taut and senses heightened, ready for him to make a move. She circled him, wanting to make a move, yet held off. Needing to see if he would have the balls big enough to advance on her.

He lunged at her, dagger in hand. A wide smile curved upon her lips. He did not disappoint her. She easily sidestepped his unskilled move. He was slow and unsure on his feet. He never took care of his dirty deeds. All he seemed to be able to do was beat on the innocent.

"Is this all ye are capable of? I am very disappointed. I had hoped for more," she taunted as she closed in. "My turn," she hissed.

She struck hard and fast. Sir Argyle never saw it coming. Stumbling backwards a few steps before he caught his balance.

"Are we having fun yet?" she whispered over his shoulder.

She held there behind his back long enough for him to regain his senses. She got the reaction she wanted. He whirled on her quicker than she had anticipated, grasping her upper left arm. She glanced at her arm; it seemed apparent to her he was applying extreme pressure. Not that she felt pain.

"Is this good enough, ye bitch? Ye at my mercy now," he spat as he tightened his grip on her.

Serena knew what he was going to do, and she was ready for it. He pulled her in close to him, giving him the ability to grab both her arms.

It is just like a man to use his brute force to get his way, she thought to herself as she went flying.

Lifting her off her feet, he flung her aside as if she were nothing more than a small kitten. Serena rotated her body in a way to help slow her momentum. Once in the position, she threw her legs up and over her head, causing her body to arch to correct itself. Landing on her feet in a low crouch, ready to pounce, she slowly straightened in her stance.

"What in the bloody hell are ye?" he asked in a tone hinting at fear.

"I am yer worst nightmare," she said in a very sweet tone as she stalked the ground between them. Still talking, she neared him. "To make myself clear, when I say yer worst nightmare, I am talking about the ones that wake ye from yer sleep," she said as her fangs fully extended for him to see.

Seumas watched from a distance, keeping clear so as not to get in the way. She fought better than most men he knew. He was so utterly occupied with the scene before him that he did not see William move to Lady Kari's side. He held her with such gentleness, love, and compassion. He knew he wanted the same with this goddess before him.

It was time for him to put a stop to this ill-matched pair facing off.

The thrill of the hunt rushed through her veins. It felt odd to her, a feeling that should've been a natural reaction. Yet it was not. She had spent too many years as a pet to mortal laws. She had already killed two souls out of a need for survival. One more to save innocents should balance her karma.

At the very same moment, Seumas moved in. She attacked swiftly and deadly. She sprang at the man with nay a weapon in hand. Her face was hidden from view as their bodies smashed into each other, fists swinging at one another. His blows hit their mark on her soft body, he saw red. Nay man should hit a woman, but this swine was no man. Nay, he was a wife beater. A coward draped in the flesh of a man.

A roar of anger pierced the air, and then all eyes were on him, all but the two fighting. They never stopped. Within no time, he was on the outside of the duelling pair, circling. Then, he heard her voice as clear as day. The pitch of her voice was like honey, smooth and sweet.

A grin curved his lips. His woman. *Mine*.

She had been made for him. He liked the thought of her belonging to him. She would be his. There was no doubt about that.

"My turn," she murmured.

Striking hard at his breastplate, Serena followed his body as he stumbled backward, throwing jabs at his midsection. Each blow knocked the breath out of his body. Seumas could hear him trying to regain his breathing in between hits. She never let up, did not even show signs of tiring. Her next hit drew blood.

" 'Tis not as easy to beat a woman when she can defend herself, is it?" she hissed. "Now, it is yer time to be afraid and know death is knocking at yer door. The difference between ye and yer wife from this day on is, that Lady Kari is going to live a long and healthy life without fear. Ye, sir, are going to die today, and I am yer executioner," she proclaimed.

He turned red with anger as he struggled to speak. "Ye are a dead wench," he said, gasping for air. "As for my wife, she is not leaving anywhere." He took a threatening step toward Kari. Coming to a halt as William stepped in front of his woman, his body hard and rigid, ready to attack. "Who the hell are ye?" he spat.

"Somebody who as well wishes to kill ye," he snarled.

"Stand in line, friend. He is mine. This day is his last," Serena said with a smile.

Sir Argyle backed away from William and right into Serena.

"Are ye ready to meet yer maker?" she whispered into his ear. "I was willing to walk away with yer wife and have her break the spell ye have on her. Then, ye had to go and hit her. So, now, ye die, and by doing so, the hold ye have over these lands will disappear as well."

That statement got the reaction she wanted.

"How do ye know about that?"

"I found the scroll hidden in yer study. That is the last ye will see of it."

Fear was running deep inside him; she could smell it on him. Serena finished him off, and before his body hit the ground, she was at Kari's side.

Serena's senses heightened. She could smell the blood dripping from his cuts, and she wanted to feed. Her hunger was still not under control, still a threat to these people. It was the same feeling she'd had each and every day in Henderson. The dangerous predator, ready to hunt, was still hungry, and that hunger did not allow her fangs to retract. Reining in her body's demands.

"Are ye all right?"

Her response was a quick nod of her head. Still unable to open or move her jaw without it causing pain.

"Is this the man ye told me about?"

Another quick nod came.

"Thank the heavens for him coming here. Ye are safe now. Thank ye, Meg, for looking after Lady Kari and for cleaning the blood from her. Ye are a good person to have handy."

Meg absolutely beamed at her, as if she had been given the greatest of praise. She guessed, in a way, she had.

"Please excuse me. I need fresh air."

With that, she started for the door. Instead, Serena found herself face-first into a wall—a very male brick wall. She stepped back with all intention to go around him, but he stepped in her path yet again.

"Excuse me, sir," she said as she tilted her face upward. Her breath caught in her throat. "Ye."

Her body instantly grew hot, and the mere smell of him got her wet. She could feel her nipples tighten in answer to what she felt.

"Milady," he said in a voice as rich as cream.

His eyes locked on hers. The intense look within them only added to her yearning for him.

He leaned in close to her ear, making it impossible for anyone else to hear. "I did not think ye to be real. I began to wonder if I only imagined ye out of my own needs." He spoke the words to her, all the while breathing her in. His cock grew thick and rock hard. His sac pulled up high, begging for release from the sweet smell of her. His hand swept up to touch her face, as he was desperate to feel her creamy-white skin under his hand.

Serena was unable to utter a word. She stood there, gaze locked on his. Heat engulfed her from the look he was giving her. The attraction she felt toward this god of a man could not become anything more than a very sexual fantasy. She stepped away from him, frantically needing space between them.

"Milord, do ye know this lady?" asked William. "I have need to thank her for what she has done."

The sound of William's voice pulled him free of his trance. Realising he had yet to introduce himself, he looked for a way to make this situation less awkward.

He cleared his throat before he spoke. "I am Seumas MacIver, milady," he said with a nod of his head.

"I'm no lady, sir. My name is Serena Wulff. A pleasure to meet you, Seumas," she murmured as she held out her hand, intending to shake hands.

Instead, he gently took it in his hand and brought it to his lips. A wave of heat radiated from those sensual lips and penetrated her skin. He stepped away from her with a grin on his handsome face as he chuckled. He knew the effect he had on her, and like an alpha male, he revelled in that knowledge.

"I do not mean to laugh at ye, mistress. However, I would have to agree with ye. You are most definitely not a common lady. You are a lady all the same. Lady Serena," he said, looking her over, "we have nay known a woman like ye before. Ye fight with no fear in yer heart. The courage and skill shown today is worthy of any man."

"Thank ye, Seumas. William, I will now give the care of Lady Kari over to your capable hands. It was by happy chance ye came here today. I was going to take Kari over to yer holding. You have saved me a trip. Good day, gentlemen." With that spoken, she darted for the door.

Seumas and William had a look of confusion on their faces as they watched Serena flee.

"What does she think she's doing? Better yet, where does she think she is going?" Seumas asked of William.

"I do not know, milord. Ye'd better go and fetch her back before she gets too far. I will get my woman ready to leave."

He took off, sprinting fast out of the keep doors.

Chapter Twelve

Serena blasted out of the doors and into the sunlight. Causing her to pause giving her eyes time to adjust. Tears rimmed her lids as the sting intensified for the briefest of seconds. This was nothing new to her. Her body was going through changes, reverting to the predator within.

Gathering her wits about her, she ran for the gates and to freedom. She wiped at her eyes as she continued to move. No time to waste. Someone was coming.

She went a great distance, no longer able to view the keep. The person still pursued her, still gave chase. Whoever was following did not let up. She could hear the person closing the distance between them. She stopped dead in her tracks. Causing their body to slam hard into hers. It should've sent her reeling from the pure force of impact. She should've been able to lose this mortal, yet she couldn't, and so stopping had become her only option.

Serena squared off with the person, who was now too close for comfort. Taking a deep breath, she straightened to her full height and looked him in the eyes.

"Why are ye following me?" she asked in a tone not hiding her anger.

Watching with the eyes of a predator, she noticed he was struggling to regain his normal breathing. Her eyes settled on his carotid artery, pulsing strong under tender flesh. Big mistake. Her hunger boiled over the edge. She had fought hard against sinking her fangs in and drinking her fill of Sir Argyle. The smell of this man had her mouthwatering for his blood. Hissing through clenched teeth, she pressed him once more.

Seumas had yet to answer her. He stood as still as possible. She had leaned in, and he felt her breath warming his flesh. Her scent penetrated his nostril cavity, tickling at his senses. She smelled of sweet vanilla and honey. His eyes drifted shut as dreams flashed in his mind. Ones of soft creamy-white skin pressed up against his hard, tanned flesh, rubbing him in a purely provocative invitation. Wanting nothing more than what his dreams offered him, and he wanted it with this woman.

Hissing in frustration, she found herself drawn to him. The blood flowing in his veins had a pure, untainted aroma, her eyes drifted shut. She didn't need to feel her fangs to know they had extended. She could do this—bite into his flesh and drink of him. Suck the blood out of his body. To experience Seumas's life force pour down her throat, filling her belly. The thought of it made her dizzy with delirium. She swayed, and her eyes closed on that thought.

"Ye need to get far away from me—now," she demanded.

Those words slapped him awake. "I am nay going anywhere without ye at my side," he murmured as he very gently ran his fingertips over her collarbone and down the slope of her breast. "Ever since I saw ye, I wanted ye. I grew hard with that wanting. Did nay even know if ye existed."

"Ye, sir, are the reason I am here," she said as she pulled the blade out. "This cursed thing brought me here, and now, I have no way back to my time." She walked off, talking to herself, mumbling under her breath. Replacing the jewel-encrusted blade back in the waistband of her gown, not realising that she said it out loud.

Why am I complaining? I should be happy to be here. It takes care of my problem. I needed to be me, and being in this place—hell, in this time for that matter—would allow it. There's only one matter I have to right—how in God's name do I communicate with Kimmie and Tom? Hells bells! Who the hell am I kidding? This is not my only issue here. I need a place to stay. Maybe Milton would allow me to stay in his barn.

Seumas gazed at her in complete and utter wonder. He found her absolutely bewitching. Not only was she mumbling to herself, but she had also completely forgotten all about him. By her doing so, he learned she had nay place to stay. Milton's barn. The woman was actually talking about sleeping in a barn. Serena had been made for him. Beauty, courage, and strength—qualities any real man desired in a woman, and he wanted her for himself.

"Pardon me, Lady Serena. I can help ye with at least one of yer problems, as ye put it."

"I am not a lady," she hissed. "And what is it ye think ye can help me with? I believe ye have already done enough, thank ye very much. I would not be in this position if it was not for yer cursed blade."

"Aye, ye are a lady. You are not going to stay in Milton's barn. Ye will be staying in my keep with me," he purred in a husky tone.

"Did ye say I'm staying with ye in your keep?"

"I did. Let me clarify what I mean for ye. Ye will be staying in my bedchamber with me," he said with a sexual grin.

"We do not know each other at all, and ye are suggesting I stay in your keep. Not just stay in yer keep, but also in yer bedchamber. Do I have this right?" she asked in a curious tone.

"Aye, milady, 'tis what I have suggested," he answered as he moved in to inhale the scent of her hair.

The intensity in his eyes spoke of his sexual need for her. She would have seen it in him from across a crowded nightclub. Hell, she could've smelled the lust radiating from his body, even with all the heated bodies rubbing on each other on the dance floor. Pure male. He was a man who would not go unnoticed. Not able to resist, she ran her fingers across his soft, full lips. The softness they offered had her licking her lips in invitation. Serena watched in awe as Seumas's eyes turned a darker blue as the sexual heat between them grew tenfold.

A growl rumbled deep in his throat from the mere sight of her pink tongue moving across her lips. He did not need any further invitations. Seumas pulled her hard up against his body, claimed her mouth in a firm, demanding kiss. Which she was more than willing to answer in like.

His tongue rubbed over hers, sending shivers down her spine. He felt her tremble in his arms and loved the way it felt. For the briefest of seconds, the whole of her body moved against his. Adjusting his hold, he deepened the kiss to satisfy his hunger.

Serena moaned her pleasure. The pressure of his lips, hands, and the smooth, sweet, spicy taste of him had her wanting more. Essential she have more of this man in her arms. She yearned for it right now. She climbed up his rock-hard body, wrapped her legs around his waist, ground down on his hard shaft, desperate to feel the full length of him. He grunted his approval as his hands slid down her back to support her firm bottom. Allowing her to fully feel his throbbing manhood.

Breaking the feverish kiss, he said in a dark sexual growl, "We need to stop this play right now. I fear I won't be able to stop from taking ye."

"I have no intention of stopping, Seumas," she purred. "I want this. I need this. I want ye deep inside me, filling me. Ye do not need to worry about me. My virginity was lost long ago."

A desperate groan of longing escaped his lips at her declaration. He had to be strong. They had to cease this play.

"Nay, Serena. I can nay dishonour ye in this way, milady," came out in a husky tone.

"Once more, I am not a lady. No shame in us seeking pleasure from each other's bodies. Especially when I have a more than willing partner," she said as her thighs tightened about his waist. Causing his cock to jump in response to the delightful pressure.

"As ye wish, milady," was all he said as he looked around for a place that would offer more cover.

Yet it was apparent the woman in his arms did nay care if any saw. That knowledge showed how right she was for him. He spent his life for others, not her. She spent her life for herself. Taking all this world had to offer. They were perfect for one another, counterbalancing each other. He made his way into the nearby wooded area. It would have to do. He couldn't wait any longer to take her body.

Serena did not have to be told what he was doing. She knew well enough to know they were making their way into the woods. She was happy he wanted her as much as she desired him. Wondering why he had yet to ask her about her fangs. An urge so primitive ran through her to rub them over his soft flesh. She desired him. He should know what she was before they had relations.

"Hell, I'm not going to get off today," she whispered to herself. That thought cooled her blood a little, enough for her to get control of her emotions, fangs and all.

Seumas felt the change in her body immediately. Stopping, pressing her up against a nearby tree, spreading her wide, he rubbed his hard shaft firmly against her.

Letting her head roll back, she whimpered in her pleasure. This was the sound he had longed to hear. As quickly as the change in her body had appeared, it disappeared. Thanking the heavens for the change in her body, he needed her. For he knew he would not be able to stop himself now. The fire in him raged too fiercely.

Her ankles locked behind him gave her the ability to pull the hem of her gown up, freeing the lower half of her body. Well, almost completely. There was still the barrier her panties offered. She prayed for him to solve their dilemma, closing her eyes as the warmth of his body touched the core of her.

He felt her quiver as he ran his hands up her slim thighs and reached for her bottom. The smoothness of her skin had him itching to see all of her flesh, to feel the firmness of her taut posterior and the heaviness of each breast.

"Woman, ye have too much cloth on ye," he said in a gruff, husky voice. The very tone of it hardened her nipples more so.

She pulled the blade that had brought her here, sliding it between them. "Let me help ye resolve that," she murmured as she placed the hilt of the blade in his hand.

He needed no further prompting from his woman. Taking the blade with the skill of a master, he cut through the lacy fabric with ease. When he dropped the knife to the ground beside them, the fabric fell away, exposing her folds to him. The moist heat from between her legs filled the air around them. Watching through hooded gaze, he inhaled the very scent of her, taking in the wild look that took over his eyes. The look in his eyes drove her over the edge.

"I want ye in me now. Right now," she said in a sharp command.

A growl tore from his throat. "Aye, mistress. How would you like it—slow and easy, or hard and fast? What would ye have of me, Serena? Or shall we not think, just act on that primitive urge?"

She did not answer in an audible way. Instead, she reached for his kilt hem, pulling it up, freeing him. Stroking his hard cock with her hand, liking the way he felt. The soft, smooth skin to the hard steeliness of his manhood caused her core to heat up even more, it jumped in her hand, and that wanting to feed her need for more. Wrapping her hand around his shaft, testing his thickness , had goosebumps running up and down her flesh.

"Oh my, ye most definitely are all male," she purred as she joined their bodies with such force that the whole of her body quivered instantaneously around him.

Seumas groaned his pleasure. She was bold, beautiful, and dripping for him. The softness of her hand drove him over the edge. The sheer force with which she had taken him within her body broke any restraint he had held. She shuddered in his arms. Loving the way it felt, he wanted more of it and of this woman in his arms.

His control snapped, and instinct took over. Taking hold of her waist, he pumped deep inside her, burying the full length of his shaft to the hilt.

"Heaven," he murmured as he began to move with an even greater urgency.

Their moans rang out together, echoing within the woods.

Serena felt every thrust go deeper than the last. Savouring the way he felt as each of her muscles contracted around his hard cock, she moved with him, riding him with as much force as possible. Matching him thrust for thrust with that of her own need. Dropping her head on his shoulder gave her better access to his neck to lick, bite, and kiss. Dragging her tongue across his skin caused an entirely new sensation. Saltiness coated her tongue, driving her a little more over the edge. Arching her back gave her what she wanted. He was so deep in her, and now, they were truly one. He knew how to use the equipment God had given him.

He tugged her breasts free, drawing one very taut nipple into his mouth. Rolling it seductively between his tongue and palate of his mouth, sucking and lapping gently on the rosy bud. The slight pull of her nipple sent her spiraling over the edge. Her body tightened and pulsated around his rigid shaft, a moan of pleasure ripped from her throat. With a few more powerful thrusts, he followed suit, burying himself deep within her body. Serena rocked on him, ensuring his full climax, loving the way he felt within her.

Seumas gently eased Serena back to her feet as his sexual haze relaxed its hold over him, pinning her between his body and the tree. Embracing her in his arms, loving the way she fit against his body. The intimacy he shared with this goddess was like none he had ever felt, not even with his wife. He wanted more of this, of her, and he wanted it soon.

Chapter Thirteen

Serena welcomed his embrace, his scent. This was what she had missed in her modern life—warmth, tenderness, and love. She had never wanted anything as much as she wanted this from this man. Sorrow struck her with the knowledge that she would live forever, he would die, and she would be abandoned once again. She could be cold to what she was feeling. She could walk away and just chalk it up to a one-night stand. However, it would be a lie. A lie she did not want to continue. He deserved the truth. She would give it.

Taking a deep breath, she forced herself to push away. "Seumas," she whispered.

He looked down at her, gazing deep into her eyes. "Aye, mistress?"

"What ye want cannot be. I am not the person ye think I am." Pausing, she searched for the right words. Not able to find them, she would just say it. Taking a step back, she spoke. "Seumas, I am not a normal female," she stated, taking one more step back. "For this reason, I won't come to yer keep."

The puzzled expression on his face told her much.

"Did ye hear me, Seumas?" She saw pain shadowed deep in his eyes. Hurting him was not what she had wanted. Yet that was exactly what would happen if she stayed. "I am sorry for the pain I have caused ye. Ye won't feel agony from me again. I am truly sorry." With this, she leaned in to give him a kiss. Brushing her lips over his neck feeling his pulse steady and strong. "Good-bye."

"Where do ye think ye be going?" he demanded, pulling her hard up against him. "Ye do nay have to tell me ye are not a normal woman. 'Tis what I like about ye," he said as he smelled her hair. "Ye are coming with me even if I have to carry ye there."

"Seumas, ye still do not understand. So, I am going to show ye what I mean."

She gathered her vigour to turn around. He was going to run once he saw what she truly was. Running her tongue over her teeth, she felt each point of her fangs. Her fangs wouldn't be the only detail he noticed. Facial features transformed ever so slightly, enough for one to see the predator. It brought back the memories of villagers fleeing in terror. She had not blamed them. She remembered the old life. The humans were food, walking blood sacs, cattle, and they hunted them as such. Serena wanted to revert back to her old self. No treatments, no shots, no nothing. To become a creature of the dark once more. To feed as one was supposed to, only this time, she would do it with humanity. She was stalling, and she knew it. Now was the time for her to face the man she had shared the best sex ever with.

"This is what I am, Seumas," she murmured, facing him.

"What are ye speaking of, lass? Ye are magnificent. Aye, I know ye are nay like other women," he said as he rubbed the back of her hand.

The hurt he felt disappeared as he watched her struggle with the words she wanted to say. He saw the concern on her face.

"Look at me. Do ye not see what's staring ye in the face?" Sighing in her frustration, she tried to make him see.

"Lass, do ye believe I have nay taken note of the fangs in ye mouth?" he asked with a smile on his face. "Milady, I saw them as well as felt them on my flesh. 'Tis of nay matter to me. I still desire ye. I have waited for what seems like a lifetime for these feelings ye have given me, and I will nay let it go." He observed her whiten ever more so.

"Ye do not care that I am different, do ye?" she said as tears ran freely down her cheeks. Hastily wiping at her tears, trying in a desperate manner to remove the evidence that sat upon her skin, she was unable to stop the floodgates that opened.

He was accepting her for who she was. He still didn't know the full truth about her. She threw her arms around him. No man had ever accepted her for who and what she was. Only immortal acknowledged immortal.

He held her close as she silently cried, rubbing her back tenderly. The tears she shed pained him, enraged him. Had no man ever loved the lass? There had to be a husband or a secret lover in her life. She was no virgin. Serena made love like a wild siren, like a woman who held nothing back. These tears showed she never truly had love.

Tilting her chin up, he gently wiped away the wet. "Come, lass. Let us make our way back to the keep. We have friends awaiting us."

Serena silently let him lead her back to the dark keep, joining the few friends she had made.

He did not realise how far she had run until they headed back. He called upon his magic to keep pace. She fought like a skilled warrior, had the speed of the gods, and the heart of a genteel lady. He could fall in love with her without even taking note. There were many parts to this woman, and he intended to explore them all—inside and outside of the bed chamber. Christ, he needed to get to the keep now, before he took her once more. The images of her pushed up against the tree, riding him, was far too fresh in his mind.

"Sweetling, do ye think ye are up to running back to the keep? At this rate, we shan't be back by midday."

Seumas regarded her with such compassion. She could run around the world if it pleased him.

"I'm much better, thank ye. It was very thoughtful of ye to ask. To answer yer question, yes, I am more than capable of running. I did not think I'd gotten far. I only stopped because I was unable to lose ye." She gave him a puzzled look. "How was that possible? I am faster than any human. Ye kept up with me. How?" she questioned.

"There's nay time for answers, lass. We must get moving if we wish to reach my holding in a timely manner. I shall give ye all the answers ye wish once at my keep," he said calmly.

He would give her the truth even if it caused him pain. First, he planned to use the crystal to see into the heart of her. Before he went any further with this newfound relationship.

Desiring to lighten the mood between them, she took on a more playful attitude. She gave him the coyest look she could manage right before she slapped him on his very taut ass as she ran away. "I bet ye I can get there before ye." She giggled.

He stood there, watching as she vanished. Coming out of his shock, he called upon his magic. As he took off at an inhuman pace, his magic was the only ground to his body. It took a little bit of time to catch up with her. When he did, he could her hear playfully teasing him.

"Seumas. Seumas, darling, come and get me. Catch me if ye can."

Sweet heavens, he loved the sound of her voice. He heard himself laughing as he followed her.

Serena slowed enough for him to get close, taunting him with her body. At the very last second before he would grab her, she would race off again. Their play continued the whole way back to the gloomy keep. They stopped to touch, pet, and kiss one another along the way. To feel the sexual energy radiating off each other. She swore, that if ye looked closely, ye see sparks flying between them.

Their mood changed quickly as the shadows of the keep came into view. Even now, with Sir Argyle's death, evil lingered, shrouded in an eerie veil, awaiting a new master. It would take time for the evil to leave the land and the holding itself.

Chills ran down her spine as she entered the gloom. Her body was aware of the evil surroundings she found herself in once more. Things were already different with the locals. They seemed relaxed and very happy. Meg beamed with life as she helped her family and friends. Then, there was Lady Kari and William. He held her with such love and longing in his eyes. She fit in his arms so naturally. She belonged in his embrace. Even with all of this, it was not the love she saw right now, but the pain expressed on her face. Serena would have to scour the land for a plant root or herb of some sort to help ease the pain. Lady Kari needed narcotics. Hell, she would even benefit from some really good weed.

"Pardon me, Lady Serena. Might I enlist yer help with my beloved? I but seek a moment with Seumas," asked William. He must inform his lord of what had happened here the last few days, before Sir Argyle's death.

"Of course, William. I am more than happy to look after her until ye return," murmured Serena as she smiled at Kari.

Chapter Fourteen

Seumas watched and took note of the way his woman assisted Lady Kari. His heart lurched in his chest. His hands clenched on his sporran, containing all of his hopes and the answers to his questions. He desperately wanted to see into her heart to fully understand this woman.

"Milord," William called out. "I learned much about what had taken place here," said William as he approached Seumas.

It had taken Seumas some time to catch and bring back Lady Serena. He found himself wondering what had taken place between them. His lord seemed completely taken by this woman. There was definitely something spectacular about her. It was easy to see how he could become infatuated with her. She had mystical qualities about her.

"Tell me what took place here that caused Lady Serena to take his life," he said, not taking his eyes off her. "Meg informed me that Sir Argyle had brutally beaten Lady Kari last eve. Meg had gone to check on her mistress before retiring for the night, and all was well, everything in its place. Lady Kari sat before the fire without a mark on her. Seeing all was well, she headed out to get her much-needed rest. Lady Serena and Lady Kari were attempting to leave the keep when Sir Argyle hit her once more. It seems as well that Lady Serena had but been here a few days. While she might freely leave this place, Kari could not. She planned to take her with her. 'Twas when we came in to find Lady Serena facing off with this dog," he said, not liking the taste it left in his mouth. "I wanted to take his life. It should have been me. Not a woman. 'Tis nay right."

"Ah, there, there, friend. 'Tis best ye did nay take his life. We did not come here to kill but to free a woman from her captor. Nor had we been informed about the beating she had taken. If there were witnesses to his crimes and cruelty to the people in his care, they did nay come forward. All it would have taken was for one to speak up, proclaiming Sir Argyle was defending himself. Demanding justice," he said, turning to William. "Ye know what would happen then, don't ye?" He could only hope no one would come forth. Not like what would happen to Serena and Lady Kari if one should speak up.

"I have not thought 'bout what would happen. We need to keep an ear to the ground. 'Twill be the only way to keep them safe," he said, looking over to Lady Kari.

She had been through hard times. Now, all that was behind her. This was how he planned to keep it.

"William, 'tis time to go. Gather what is necessary for your lady friend. Only take the necessities. Make sure she understands, William. Only what she can carry."

"Kari, I believe it's time for us to leave. I am sorry. Do ye mind if I call ye Kari or perhaps Kar? Ye can tell me which ye like once ye are able to speak again," said Serena as she helped Lady Kari fix her gown. "Better yet, ye can write yer responses down for me."

The smile she had on her face disappeared as Lady Kari shook her head.

"Ye can write, can't ye?"

She shook her head one more time. "Well then, we are going to fix that. Can ye read?"

Serena was relieved this time when she nodded.

"That's really wonderful. It will save time."

This is good, she thought to herself. *Definitely positive.*

She would need a distraction from her hunger. Who was she kidding? She had to stay far away from Seumas.

Lost in thought, she did not notice William come over and carry Kari into the keep. Serena moved at once to follow them inside, only to be stopped by a pair of very strong, muscular hands on her shoulders.

"Nay, lass, they won't be but a moment," he whispered in her ear.

The warmth of his breath caressing against the lobe of her ear sent chills down her spine, causing her to take a deep breath.

Dear God, she wanted him right now. Her blood raced, pupils dilated, fangs extended. She could feel his heart beating powerfully and steady against her back. Closing her eyes, she counted the beats. So very strong. The heat coming off his body was driving her mad. She could walk away from him. In fact, she should walk away. Instead, she found herself pushing her backside up against him, rubbing and grinding. His body responded swiftly to what she offered. He felt rock hard, so very large and so very male, pressed up against her.

Turning to face him, leaning in on her tippy-toes, "Seumas," his name said in a very husky tone. "I want to take ye into my mouth and taste the saltiness that is ye," she whispered as she gazed deep into his mesmerising eyes.

A smile of pure, sensual wickedness graced his face. How he wished to act on that invitation. To go into one of the outer buildings to tup their brains out. He wanted nothing more than to throw her over his shoulder like a barbarian. Stride to the nearest building and tear off her gown, exposing her to him. A gown which revealed far too much of her soft flesh. He ran the back of his hand over the swell of her breast, groaning in his desperation to touch more of her.

"Nay the time. I'm going to take ye up on that offer at a later time," he said as he moved around her. " 'Tis time to go, lass. Come. We ride together."

"How far is yer land?" Hoping it was close, her thirst growing rapidly, she knew that, soon, she would not be able to control herself.

They found William and Lady Kari already mounted on their horses, ready and eager to ride away from this dark place. Their horses awaited them. He whistled three low notes, and in response, his horse trotted over to him. A magnificent specimen, muscular in frame and so tall that the horse towered over her. The beast's flanks showed the strength within. The sleek, dark coat shone beautifully. Which left the smaller, less muscular horse for her.

"What's the horse's name?" she asked, reaching for him.

Serena neared his horse, and it reared itself upright on its hind legs in an attempt to protect itself and that of his master. The horse felt and knew a predator when one was near. Before she could try to correct the situation, Seumas stepped in. He was using a firm hand as he dealt with his mount. She did not want the horse to be disciplined harshly.

"Lass, are ye hurt? I am lost as to what riled him. Roderick never acts thus."

The look in his eyes said it all for Serena. She understood what had happened. Somehow, she would have to make Seumas understand. Roderick was reacting to the predator within her.

"Lass, I am truly sorry. Ye are unharmed," he asked with great trepidation as he looked her over.

"Dearest heart, don't fret. There is not a scratch on me. However, I am not happy about having to ride the small mare. I prefer to ride, Roderick," she murmured as she took the reins.

Before he could protest, she had the reins to Roderick and was on his back. They all watched in horror as the horse reared and bucked, trying desperately to throw her.

Feeling the beast under her starting to tire, she leaned forward to its ear. "Now, Roderick, ye have tried to unseat me, but I have held on. I do not wish to harm ye. Ye see and feel the predator within me. This I cannot change. So, hear me now. Ye are safe. Do ye understand?"

With this said, Roderick calmed down. Tossed his head to the side as he pranced over to the stables, in a way of giving her an answer.

"I see ye understand, but I cannot ride ye. Ye need time to fully trust me."

Dismounting, she headed inside. The cold, musky air filled her lungs. Horses lined the stalls, all but two. Walking down the line of the caged animals, every one of them snorting and stomping their hooves out of fear. Desperate to escape this dark place and the danger of her. Much like her, they, too, wanted freedom.

"Seumas, what is Lady Serena doing?"

Hell, he had no clue what she was doing. Before he could answer, she burst out of the stable doors on a horse strong enough to withstand the weight of three full-grown men. Was she mad? Bloody hell, she must be. She was riding bareback. This horse could kill her, and why was she riding bareback? Did she nay care 'bout her life? He was going to have a very strong discussion with her, and if that did not work, then he would put her over his knee. Seumas liked the thought of taking her over his knee her bare backside against his hand. Perhaps he would still give her a little slap on her arse when he had her in his bed.

Serena held no sign of fear on her face, only pure joy. The type of happiness that was contagious. She did not require his protection, so why was he acting this way?

"Seumas, I am ready to go now that I have a proper mount and not that small mare over yonder, which looks as if it could barely hold the weight of an infant," she said, winking at him.

William's laughter touched her ears, widening her smile.

Riding out the gates, Seumas realised they had company. It seemed the whole of the village was coming with them. A steady line of horse-drawn wagons and carts flowed out of the gate. The younger and healthier walked beside the wagons, assisting the elderly. Children ran free, playing and chasing one another. Laughter floated in the air. Their little faces lit up with joy. This had to be the first time for them to be free. He could almost envision his son running and playing with these children. He would love to have another child. Be able to have the experience of bouncing his babe on his knee. His heart ached with longing. He glanced over to where Serena rode and wondered if she wanted children. Mayhap there was still a chance for him and his dream.

Turning his mount, he headed for the closest wagon. Intending to have a little chat with the man to see what his intentions were. He did not need more tenants or land work. Yet he would consider taking all in, if needed, sure he would find work for all.

"Sir, where do ye think ye are headed to?" he asked out of curiosity, knowing what the response would be.

"We go with ye and our mistress, Lord Seumas. If that is all right with ye, milord?" he said with a look of hope in his eyes. "We can nay stay here. 'Tis nay safe for us. Somebody will have to pay for his death, and we do nay wish it to be us," he said on a sigh.

"Do nay fret over this. Ye are all welcome to live and work on my land, if ye wish," he said with a smile as he rode away, swiftly moving to William to inform him of their company.

They would not be moving as fast as they both wished.

Chapter Fifteen

The excursion back to his land was slow. Slower than William and he liked it. The two days of hard riding gave way to frequent stops. The old and very young need rest more often. He wanted to urge them, to compel them to keep moving forward. Not wanting to come off as a tyrant, he found himself easing into the pace. They would reach his land soon enough. He got hard, thinking about the coupling they would share in and out of his bed. Planned on spending days locked in his chamber, pleasuring her in every way he knew how. Filling her with pleasure and his seed.

He watched William and Lady Kari sitting together under a tree as a fire was made for the night. William did not so much as attempt to kiss her. Seumas knew he did not trust himself with just kissing. He understood that feeling. It had been two very long days of not touching, kissing, or bedding his woman. Every time she neared him, his senses drowned in her scent—the sweet smell of vanilla honey. How he loved honey. He wanted nothing more than to drizzle the sweet, sticky syrupy substance over her flesh, to suck and lick every drop off her soft body. To hear her every moan and soft mewling made. To feel each touch of her soft hands running up and down his body. To have her nails bite his flesh as he pounded in to her heated channel as he hits that special place deep inside every woman.

His mind kept wandering, no matter how he tried to attend to his duties. Giving in to his urge, he went in search of Serena. With each respite, she seemed to vanish from sight. Compelled to walk after riding for most of the day. He left her to her solitary walks. Knowing he could not be trusted to be alone with her. This night was different. He would not let her wander in the dark alone. Darkness offered cover from prying eyes. Cover for him to give in to his desire.

Hunger raged within her, pushing her to her limits. Praying to rest for the night, she had about jumped for joy when Seumas announced they would be stopping. The smell of blood was getting harder to withstand by the second, blood so clean that she wanted to drag an unwilling soul aside and drain them dry. To feel her fangs pierce their untainted flesh and lick the salt from their skin. She would have to make do with whatever animals she found in the nearby wooded area. She would not take what was not willingly given, not again. Serena was in the woods tracking and not finding a single sign of animals, every creature vanished from the woods. She was not able to go far in search of them, and they felt a predator was near, so they scattered to the wind. She would have to bide her time, for now, the best she could.

"Ah… there ye are, lass. I've been looking for ye," he said as he wrapped his arms around her waist, breathing in the scent of her hair.

She could hear the pure joy he took in this simple gesture.

"I decided I would join ye on yer walk. I've been lacking in me duties to ye, letting ye wander alone at every stop. Eve's upon us, and I've a fierce need to see ye in the moonlight."

Dear God… he knew how to get her blood boiling over with lust. The walks fixed two needs for her. First, gave her the chance to try to find nourishment. Second, put distance between her and the humans' blood. Until she could feed, it was best if she kept isolated.

"I think it best if ye went back with the others, Seumas." She gulped as she tried not to think about his blood, but it was too late. "Seumas," she said with a wealth of emotions laced in his name as she stared into his eyes. "I could hypnotise ye to get what I so desperately require. However, I am not going to do that. Ye said ye take me as I am, so, now, I am about to put yer sentiment to the test." Everything in her screamed to glamour him, to protect her secret. Yet she could not, yearning for his trust. "I need nourishment from ye. I require ye to give of yerself willingly."

"Food's what ye seek. Ye but need to tell me what ye wish, and I would fetch it willingly, lass. Nay need to demand me away or put me under a spell. Ask me what ye would, Serena." He could feel she was trying to tell him something. She need only ask.

No way to pussyfoot around this. So, she blurted it out. "I need yer blood." That was clear enough.

His eyes widened with that statement. Yet he did not react. He still gazed upon her with loving eyes. He simply reached into his pouch and pulled out the crystal she had buried in the muddied earth. Reaching out for it, she stopped herself mid-grasp.

Seumas held the crystal as he watched her reach out. Glad to see she knew how to control her actions. Placing his other hand on her exposed skin, he focused on her. Images flowed in waves. Many of them he understood. A great deal more he nay comprehended. Even with all he saw, the blood surrounding her concerned him. He pushed aside images of blood to focus on the children—his children. They had the look of their mother in their eyes. Watching images of him and his children playing and singing "Ring Around the Rosie" warmed his heart. He could almost hear them singing the song. Almost felt their warm little hands in his. He closed his eyes as he tried desperately to rein in his emotions. He would have this. She was asking for his blood, and he would give it willingly if it got him what he had been shown.

Serena hoped for a quick decision. She could taste him already. He was so close. She did not know how it happened. Before she knew it, she tasted the salt from his flesh, blood. Her eyes flew open. Stepping back, she looked up at him with a look of horror in her eyes. What had she done?

"Oh God, Seumas... I am sorry," she said as she backed away.

The reading stopped as he felt her lick his chest, felt the coolness of her breath on him. There was a slight prick, quickly replaced by suckling. The feeling of it had his sac pulled up tight. He was about to spill his seed like some untrained boy by that one action. The sensation stopped as suddenly as it had started. He wanted it back. Looking down at her, he saw the look of shock on her face. He did not want her to be scared.

"Nay, love. 'Tis nothing to be upset about. Come back in me arms. 'Tis truly fine, my love. I understand," he said as he held out his arms. "Come, my love."

She came easily into his embrace even though he sensed the slightest of reserve within her. He could feel the tension in her body. Fear ran deep.

"I took what was not mine to take, Seumas. It shall never happen again. I understand if ye feel the need to punish me." Praying his punishment was all that happened and not torture.

She would have been dead by now in her time. Her implant reports to her captures and the Holy Order sent swiftly out to kill her. They would have shot her with silver bullets to slow her down. Then, she would have been beheaded and her body burned. Her ashes scattered to the winds and her head was added to the Holy Order's trophy case.

That was what the bars were for. She would joke about it with her friends. People on tap, as if you ordered a Bud, Miller, or an exotic dark beer with a name you were not sure you were pronouncing right.

"Why would ye think I would punish ye, lass? I would never raise a hand to any woman. Ye nay did wrong. I nay stop ye," he murmured as he looked deep into her eyes. Her voice rang clear in his head. "Give willingly. Ah, I see. What ye seek must be given and nay taken, nay matter who it is. Well then, I give of meself willingly to ye, lass, as often as ye need," he murmured in her ear, grinding against her, his smile widening in an inviting way.

His smile and the willingness he gave of himself had her wet. Serena knew fully there were a few ways she could do this. Glamour him, making the taking of his blood more pleasurable for him, or be honest about it. Honesty won the fight.

Her concentration broke as Seumas yanked her to the ground with him. She straddled him, grinding down on his hard shaft. He would have pleasure before the taking. Just maybe he would find the taking enjoyable too. Fighting for every ounce of control over her raging hunger, his blood still lingered upon her lips, teasing her senses. She could drink from him for the rest of her life and never want another. She would have to turn him.

He watched as the predator came to life within her. Even with the predator riding hard upon her, he found her to be exquisite. His breath caught in his throat as she gazed deep into his eyes. He watched even still as her features softened before him. Her lips grazed his cheek. There was softness and hunger behind those lips. Tracing the outline of his ear with her tongue, feeling the strong pulse under his delicate flesh, she sucked and tugged at his lobe as she enjoyed the sounds of pleasure coming from deep within his chest.

"I am going to make you feel things ye never thought possible my warrior," she murmured, rubbing her body against his, her nipples pebbling against his delicious sculpted physique. She felt the rumble from his growl vibrate throughout her body as it made its way to her clit. She rejoiced in the knowledge that she could drive him mad, and it pushed her to go further to be bolder. Reaching between their bodies desperate to rid him of his kilt. Her fingertips found the hem of his kilt as she slowly dragged it up his muscular thighs. The thick cords of his muscles contracting under her caresses. His intake of his breath urged her to continue as she gently rubbed his sac. She was gentle at first as she explored his heavy sac, loving the way it felt in her hand. Serena took him to the edge of his limits as she squeezed and pulled harder. Her body responded to him as his groans grew in pitch.

"Ye, my sweet temptress, has already shown me things I never thought attainable. As for yer sexual threat, it might match that of my own thoughts," he said as he freed himself from her grasp and pinned her on her back. "My turn to make ye feel, lass. For two can play this game," he murmured against her skin.

His kisses were soft, gentle caresses along her jaw that had her body humming as he made his way down her throat to the swell of her breasts as he gently nipped at them before soothing them with a kiss. Each caress and kiss and bite placed set fire to her flesh, sending her over the edge just a little bit further. This was different from their first union. Soft, warm, gentle lovemaking, yet there was still urgency under the surface. A yearning they both felt to the very core.

She had longed for a man like this for centuries, and here he was, in mediaeval Scotland. In a time she'd already lived long ago. A time she had worked hard to forget—so much blood and murder upon her hands. She did not want to think about that right now, not with his hand where it was. She stopped thinking and felt all he gave.

Seumas slid his hand down her ribs to her very tiny waist. A waist and stomach he imagined growing heavy with his bairn. He wanted to lick and kiss every inch of her very taut stomach, yet he could not, as she was still fully clothed. He desperately wanted to see her body in the moonlight. His need was going to have to wait for now, for this was not the time or the place. His gaze hooded as he reached for the hem of her gown, freeing her lower half to him. There were no stockings or garters to distract him from what he wanted, just womanly curves and lustrous smooth skin hidden under the fine fabric.

He heard her whimper as his fingers found the very core of her. Growing harder still as he felt the hot, velvety moisture seeping from her womanly lips. He played with her, driving her mad. His long, elegant fingers teased her with long, lavish strokes along her soaked folds, applying pressure in all the right areas. He caressed her with his fingertips as he worked two thick fingers into her, finding that special place where all her senses vibrated and pulsed as he thrust them deeper and deeper into her heated channel. The pressure of her feminine muscles increased on his fingers as her climax neared. The feeling of her fluttering around his ever playful fingers had him wanting more of her. He was not done with her, not yet. He wanted to taste the sweet nectar that she offered, he lowered himself further down her heat body and nuzzled into her folds. A satisfied hum crossed his lips as his tongue found the nub of her treasure. He lapped gently at first as he continued to caress her. He was lost in sweet heaven as he lapped and nibbled her nub. She moaned his name as her pleasure grew. Her hips lifted, moving wildly against him as she sought her release. A growl ripped from his throat. Time to end his self-induced torture. His body demanded release.

The force at which he joined their bodies had Serena wanting more. She felt every inch of his long, thick shaft thrusting deep into her heated core. Contracting helplessly around him with every thrust made. He took her to the heavens with each delicious caress. Begging him to go on, begging him not to stop. All he could do was pleasure her. This was all he wanted to do for the rest of his life. To hear her moan his name, feel the pressure of her sheath tighten around his shaft. He knew she was near her climax. He could hear it in her moans, felt it to the very core of him. Felt her channel flutter around his shaft. With a few more clever strokes, she plummeted over the edge.

Serena came harder than she ever had, and with that, the primitive creature came to life. Rearing up, pulling herself to the nape of his neck, and bit. The taste of his blood hit her senses, driving her over the edge once more. She felt him still as he felt the sting of her bite. Not caring what he was feeling at that moment, she needed to feed. To her surprise, he exploded inside of her as his lust spun out of control, and a groan tore from deep in his throat. He fell to his side, taking her with him. She curled into him, loving the way it felt.

Seumas tightened his grasp around his woman. He was going to become a very greedy man when it came to her and what she offered up to him. Wanting everything she had to share—body, mind, and spirit. He felt her go lax in his arms as he threw his plaid over their bodies. Her trust in him to keep her safe as she slept in the open, had him pulling her deeper into his embrace. That trust would not be broken.

"Sweet dreams, my dark angel. Sleep in the heavens, but come back to earth, as this man needs you more than life itself," he whispered in her ear. He closed his eyes and thought no more as he joined her in slumber.

Serena purred from the depth of her soul or what little soul she had left upon hearing Seumas's sweet words. Words that called to her and spoke of his desire for her. Longing he had denied himself out of fear of forgetting a family lost long ago. She understood these emotions, but she had learned centuries ago not to let them rule her. Now is the time for him to let go, for him to have and be loved again.

Chapter Sixteen

She woke in the warmth of Seumas's strong arms, and it gave her the illusion of safety. Security she longed for, the same dependability she admired in her friends' relationships. He offered it all, and she wanted it desperately. She desired a relationship with this man, as any mortals had—one full of love, laughter, and friendship. One built on mutual trust. One built on knowing your heart was safe in their care. Knowing that they would never misplace or misguide you. In her modern time her heart would have been mistreated and misplaced without a second thought about it. Hell it would have been thrown in a blender and chopped into tiny pieces. With a sigh upon her lips, she stood and dusted off her gown, wishing she had a change of clothes. Maybe she could find a burn or a river nearby to wash her body. She definitely needed to wash after their play last night, although she did not mind having his smell on her flesh, it was a scent she craved.

Seumas rose within minutes of sunrise to find himself alone. He quickly scanned the area for Serena but with no luck. She simply was not near. He headed to camp with the intent of finding her among the group. As he entered, he found most still fast asleep. Where had she gone? The answer came quickly to him. She would want to wash after their night together.

The sun barely over the horizon, he reached the nearby burn, setting all aglow. He stopped and did not dare move any farther. She stood in the water without a stitch of garment on. Her body glowed and shimmered as the droplets of water rolled down her creamy-white flesh. He watched her from afar and kept guard of his woman. It was more than that, than wanting to protect her modesty. He wanted to see all of her beauty in the early morning light, looking like a water nymph. She turned slightly, exposing more of her silhouette to him. The curves of her breasts gave way to her slim waist and a luscious bottom he wanted to bite. Water trailed down her body, and he yearned to lick and suck every droplet from her sensitive skin. He watched as she cupped water in her small hands, letting the water run down her body. His eyes followed the trail of water to the delicate neatly trimmed little black triangle of curls. Beneath the delicate curls was the core of her, and he wanted to be there once more, deep inside her sheath, her body wrapped tightly around his as she moaned her pleasure. His blood boiling over with heat and sexual energy, he needed her. He could almost taste her on his tongue as her sweet nectar ran down his throat.

"Seumas, my love, are ye going to continue watching, or do ye care to join me? Though I do have to tell ye the water's quite frigid."

Needing no further invitation, he sauntered over to her as he stripped out of his tartan. His toes curled up, and gooseflesh appeared on his skin. The water was freezing. His body warmed quickly as he pulled his woman into his arms. His manhood jumped to life as he felt her sensual body rub up against him in pure invitation.

Serena knew what she was doing to him. She smelled the lust, the sexual desire coming off of him in waves. She felt his blood quicken in his veins. Her body reacted, pupils dilated, fangs extended. Blood rushed to her head, pounding in her ears. The predator within her recognized his blood and wanted it. Not ready to give in, she rose up on her tippy-toes and kissed his soft, full lips, losing herself in the kiss. A shiver went down her back as his tongue swept across her palate. He deepened the kiss, savouring the way she shivered and pressed her body into his. The stubble on his face added to her yearning of him. How she desperately wanted to feel his five o'clock shadow on her sensitive lower region, as he nibbled on her clit as he brought her to a deliciously mind blowing orgasm.

Breaking the kiss, gasping, her body tingling with desire, she could not help but laugh. She went from a celibate cold fish to being a wanton woman. Serena wanted everything Seumas offered and then some. She wanted eternity with this man.

"Is it wise of us to start this play, Seumas?" she said, a little breathless. "I might not be able to stop if ye take me any further down this path," she murmured as she walked around his body and patted his taut ass. Her ears perked up; she heard the camp buzzing with life before he did.

He felt the change in her, not long after he heard the prattle coming from the campsite. He wanted to continue the erotic play with her. With a sigh of regret, he let the sexual haze clear from his mind. Taking a breath, trying to regain control, he found it odd that with but one kiss, she had him ready to bed her, and his proof was more than evident.

"We shall reach my holding before the day ends," he murmured softly in her ear. His breath warmed the sensitive skin there. "I will have ye in my bed by the end of this night," he said on a growl.

Serena did not say a word about the sexual threat, instead letting her body respond for her. She gazed deep into his eyes, loving what she saw within them.

"Time to dress, Seumas. They are getting near," she purred over her shoulder. "Although I do like watching yer body move very much, there is a great deal of strength in yer muscular form. Simply watching ye, I could climax," she said with a devilish smile on her face, tossing his plaid to him.

He watched her with unwavering eyes. Her lithe, feminine shape had him ready to set a hard, fast pace home. She donned her gown with a bit of a sigh. A sigh he caught all the same. He was going to remedy that. His woman would have a chamber of gowns to pick from, made by the finest of gown makers. Growling in frustration, he gazed at his woman smoothing her gown over her body. Her hands glided gently across the planes and hollows of her form, where his kisses, hands, and body should've been.

She had a look on her face that said all she was thinking.

"Come. We leave now," he growled as he grabbed her by the hand, leading her back to camp.

Serena giggled, unable to help herself. She had never felt this way before, and she loved the way it made her feel. The camp was busy with everybody working on tasks—breaking down the campsite, little ones running around and chasing each other. These were not the same people she had met just days before. They looked and felt healthier. Happier. There was a glow about them, a pure joy. It was at that moment she realised she had done the right thing by taking Sir Argyle's life. The taking of his life would never be a regret for her. Their freedom was worth the cost of the blood on her hands.

Serena spotted Kari and William at the other end of camp. Observing Kari, she noticed the limp was gone and the bruising had started to fade, no longer a deep purple. Though her jaw seemed to be causing her a great deal of pain, reminding her to seek out a plant to ease Kari's pain.

The expression on their faces made her feel as if she was invading in a private moment. Serena watched as William gently rubbed the pad of his thumb across her cheek, placing soft kisses over her eyes. Her body started to hum and moistness between her legs as she watched the interaction between the two.

I am most definitely a voyeur, she thought with a smile on her lips.

She smelled Seumas before he was even near her. She turned.

Seumas studied her as she gazed at William and Lady Kari. A look on her face spoke of what was on her mind. He found himself liking the fact that she watched such an intimate exchange between the couple. He did not expect anything less of her. She was his very wild siren. His cock jumped to life once more. He fought a strong urge to take her here and now, before all in sight. That only stirred him more.

Mayhap she would like an audience gazing upon them. Whom was he fooling? She would thrive on the undivided attention of an audience. Too bad sex with one's partner was not a spectator pastime. A laugh escaped his lips. He'd heard of such parties, hidden under the pretense of a masquerade ball, all fully aware of what the invitation implied. Women's and men's bodies intertwined with each other, all in very explicit positions. Secret orgies that were not so secret. Men on women, woman on woman, and man on man, all fucking themselves senseless. As much as there was a fierce need to share his woman, there was a more violent urge to cover what was his. She most definitely belonged to him.

Serena tilted her head to the side, regarding him with hooded lids. She knew what he was thinking. A devilish thought raced through her mind, and her nipples hardened. Her fangs extending in her excitement, there was no hiding them. She would no longer hide them from these people. They were part of her life now. She hoped that they would still accept her as a friend.

Serena was brought back to reality by a gentle touch upon her hand.

"Do nay go far, lass. I shall be but a moment. I need to instruct William and inform him of my decision," he whispered in her ear. "We'll be riding ahead of our caravan. My keep is not far if we ride hard and fast. With any luck, we might make it before supper service," he growled softly.

Chapter Seventeen

Seumas was true to his word. They rode hard and fast, and within thirty minutes, the sun would be setting. She noticed at once when they entered his land, his body seemed to relax a little bit more. Serena listened wholeheartedly to all he told her. There was no doubt he loved his land and all the people on it. His kin and clansmen alike greeted him as they rode up to the keep. His gates opened at once. Even in the dimming light, the keep was a beckon. A beckon of light spreading hope, prosperity across the land and all its inhabitants.

"Good eve, milord," said a frail looking man as he took the reins. "I will attend to the horses at once."

"Good evening, Patrick. Make sure to give them extra oats and brush them down for the night."

"Aye, milord."

"Thank ye, Patrick. After ye are done with the beasts, come to the keep for supper."

"Aye, milord. Thank ye."

"Yer welcome, Patrick. Do make sure that ye make it up to the keep."

Patrick had been through hard times in the past few months, losing function of his right leg after being brutally kicked by a horse during shoeing. The beast had belonged to his wife, and he had wished to honour her by keeping her beloved horse happy. He should've put it down long ago, only keeping the beast for sentimental reasons. He still felt the need to help Patrick, needing to make sure he was taken care of.

"Come, lass. Let me show ye to yer room."

Serena knew what he meant by the statement. Heat surged from his body. It hit her with such a force that she was drowned in his scent, and she swayed on her feet. Dear God… it felt as if he'd ravished her body, and yet he had scarcely touched her. There was most definitely something more to this man. She found herself wondering what else he was capable of making her feel.

He gave her a tour of his home before he swept her away to his room. Serena felt the pride he took in his home. She met the staff, and all showed her a great deal of respect. The kitchen still seemed to be her favourite room. Well, one of her favourite rooms. Seumas would be above all others.

However, the smells that came from the kitchen were mouthwatering, tempting her to eat. She had not eaten or tasted food in a very long time. Not because she could not eat food. There was never anything she absolutely had to taste, so she only fed on blood. Maybe, today, she would find the food to her liking.

"Milady, our chamber," he said as he ushered her into the room.

The chamber was absolutely perfect. It said much about the man. The door closed, and she heard the latch slide into place. Serena glanced over her shoulder for the briefest of seconds, Seumas was a sight to see.

"I can smell what ye want, milord," she taunted as she ran her hand over the bed. "Prithee, Seumas, answer me honestly. Is this what ye seek from me?" she whispered as she shed her gown and eased her lithe body onto the bed.

The hunger in his eyes drove her, like a blazing fire that could not be put out.

"How much time do we have, milord?"

Serena watched as he stalked across the ground between them. Eyes of a predator, eyes fixed on what he wanted, on what he would have. She knew what she was doing to him. She thrived on it, and he was almost upon her.

"Ye are a sight, my warrior. I would like ye to stop at the end of the bed, but do not touch me."

A growl rumbled from deep in his chest.

"I do love that sound coming from ye. Do as I say. Stop at the end of the bed. I will not say it again."

He knew what game was being played. He was more than willing to play it. "What would ye have of me, mistress?"

"Take off your plaid, my warrior."

"At once, mistress."

"Toss it aside."

"Does this please ye, mistress?"

"Aye, my warrior, it pleases me beyond words. Now, turn around very slowly. Show me all of you. Tease me with your body. I love to watch ye move, all muscle and strength."

"As ye wish," he said, truly enjoying this play. He turned back to face her and found her on his bed on her knees in front of him.

"Stop right there," she purred, letting her eyes roam over his body. She reached out, running her hands over his body very slowly. Her eyes drifted shut with the mere feeling of his flesh under her fingertips. Her eyes snapped open as she felt his taut body jump under her touch. "Ye like this, my warrior, don't you?" she asked as she leaned in and licked his chest. "Ye like not thinking, letting down yer guard, doing whatever pleases ye, and I give ye a great deal of pleasure."

His response vibrated through him.

He watched her through hooded lids as she lowered her hand down his body. Her small hand leaving a trail of fire down his stomach, she stopped, her hand poised just above his erection.

"What would ye have of me, my warrior?"

He chose not to answer her, instead placing his hand over hers, moving it to his throbbing manhood. He slowly started to move her hand. He was thankful she did not need any further instructions on what he wished her to do. He moaned deep and long, and his head rolled back. The pressure of her hand had him wanting more of this sweet torture. He desired more, desperate to feel the moisture of her mouth engulfing him. Gently grabbing her by her hair, he pushed her down to his thick, throbbing cock. She gave a husky laugh.

"Yes, my warrior," was all she replied.

Serena took him into her mouth, sucking and licking him into a state of frenzy. She took him deep into her throat as she slid her hand between his thighs, playing with his sac.

He almost spilled his seed at the force of the suction and the sight of her head bobbing up and down. Teasing his sac. The combination of the two weakened him. Gathering his control over his need to spill his seed, Seumas desperately desired to enjoy this play for as long as he could. There was a new sensation rubbing along his shaft. He knew at once what had joined their sexual exploration of each other. Fangs. He lost the last shred of control. He pulled himself free from her mouth and pushed her down on her back, entering her in a smooth, quick thrust. She gasped from the sheer force at which he took her. With each rock of his hips, he drove them a little more over the edge. Strumming her like a lute being played by a master musician. His hands and lips played their part in extracting her penance. A penance she would be willing to suffer through at any time. His mind went blank as his pace quickened, causing her to pant his name. Their cries of ecstasy blended together as they climaxed.

This was his heaven, and he did not want this oneness with her to end. He rolled to his side, making sure to take her with him as he stroked her hair, hair as soft as silk. To his surprise, she started to purr low and soft.

"That's very nice," she murmured. "I do like getting pets very much. Not to mention, our coupling was indeed spectacular."

"Aye, it was."

He hadn't had this connection with his late wife—may she rest in peace.

A knock at the door got both their attention. However, he loved that she did not try to hide her lithe body from his sight.

"Milord, supper is ready. 'Tis assistance needed, milord? Do ye require my services?" The last was said in a husky whisper.

A hiss passed Serena's lips. *Mine. He is mine.*

Seumas stifled the laugh he felt rising before he answered, "Nay assistance required, Belle. I will be down at once."

"Aye, milord. I shall go see to yer guest."

"That won't be necessary. I will be escorting Lady Serena to the dining hall."

"As ye wish, milord. Ye sure ye do nay need my assistance?" she asked.

Serena could hear the plea within her voice, the wanting.

" 'Tis not necessary, Belle. Thank you." Seumas turned to her and saw the possessiveness in her eyes.

Serena shook her head at herself, how quickly she was changing. To go from celibate to wanton, and now, she could throw jealousy into the mix. She had to put space between them. People were sure to notice she was not acting as one should. Serena had to change her ways from her modern way of life to one better suited to the Middle Ages.

"Seumas, this is wrong. I can nay stay in your chamber with you. I might not be from this time, but I do know that an unwed woman does not stay in a man's chamber without repercussion." She waited longer than she liked for a response. "I should have my own chamber."

"Nay. Ye will stay in this chamber with me. As for my kinsmen and clansmen alike, they know better than to speak of my private affairs. This is not up for debate, Serena."

"Yes, Seumas, it is most certainly open for debate. I will nay have yer people looking at me and talking about me behind my back. Please tell me ye understand."

Frustration came swiftly. He had to understand, not for her, but for him. It was his honour she was trying to save. She tried again.

Taking a deep breath, she tried once more. "Seumas, all I ask is a chamber where yer household staff will see me coming and going, one held for pretence."

"Ah... I believe I am coming to understand what ye are saying. Follow me, if you please."

"Can this wait until after I get dressed, my warrior?" She laughed lightly. "Should I follow ye as I am? Though yer clansmen and kinsmen alike might be more than a little shocked, but I am happy to comply."

The look he shot her was priceless. It was a mixture of laughter and mortification, as if he'd forgotten about her nudity.

Chapter Eighteen

They dined on a meal she found truly succulent. For the first time in over a century, she found herself eating and not just pushing the food around her plate. As the last of the meal was served, a squire of no more than twelve came running in. She watched as the lad approached Seumas and whispered into his ear. With a nod, the boy backed out of the room.

"It seems the caravan and William will be joining us for the eve. William must have pushed them hard," he said with a broad smile. "Shall we greet them together?" he asked as he drew her to her feet.

Together they walked the rampart overlooking the road, something was wrong. The group raced for the gates and the safety they offered. Seumas and Serena noticed someone followed.

He turned to the guards below. "On my word, open the gate. As the last of the group enters, close and bar the gate. Is that understood?" he asked in a voice used to command.

"Aye, milord."

Seumas watched as William and the party neared. In a split second of eye contact between them, he ordered the gate open and closed as the last rider entered.

Seumas and Serena stood together on the rampart, gazing out over the lower bailey. A crowd gathered in the lower bailey, mix of society from warrior to noblemen alike. Though the noblemen didn't look any nobler than that of the warlords standing with them.

"Milord, 'tis Sir Argyle's acquaintance, demanding to know who was responsible for his death," shouted William as he ran up the steps to the rampart. "I would nay give them yer woman or Lady Kari's name. Ye were right to say it takes only one to demand retribution for Sir Argyle."

"Aye, William. I did nay expect it to be so soon? We require time to come up with an adequate plan," he said, glancing at Serena. "Come, lass. I will see ye rested for the night safely in yer chamber before I talk with William."

"Do not send me to my room, Seumas, like a disobedient child ye just scolded. I am the cause of this, and I shall be the fix," she said in a tone that held authority.

"Ye may join us in my study then, but ye are to listen only. Do we understand each other?" he asked with amusement in his tone.

"Fine! I'll listen, as ye asked. However, I am telling ye now that I am going to stick my oar in."

Fire blazed in the hearth, warming and lighting the room, setting all aglow. Seumas directed them all to chairs and waited for the squire to leave once all had a drink in hand. The silence and tension in the room were thick in the air. Serena imagined this was what it must feel like for a death row inmate on his last day, awaiting his execution and praying for a stay of execution from the governor. Long moments passed before either of the men spoke. All at once, they both started to speak. The conversation went well into the predawn hours, still with no resolution in sight.

"I do not see us coming to an agreement on what must be done. William and I shall go and speak to whoever is in charge of this small army. 'Tis the only way I can see us coming up with a plan," he said, looking over at her. " 'Tis time to rest. Come, lass. William, try to get rest. Go see to yer woman."

As he escorted her out of the room, he picked her up and flung her over his shoulder, bounding up the stairs and into his chamber. Dropping her on his bed, she watched as he stripped out of his plaid, pulled the coverlet back, and slid into bed.

"Come, lass. 'Tis past time for us to seek our rest," he murmured as he pulled her close.

He was not going to give this up—her soft body close to his, warming his flesh. She belonged to him and only him.

His dreams took him to dark places, filled with war and gloominess. A field of men warring against one another blades clashing metal to metal, and men roaring in fury as they charged each other. Crimson coated the vibrant green field as claymores slashed through soft tissue and bones. Bodies littered the ground, moaning and spitting blood from their mouths as they lay there, dying on the hard, cold ground. Men clawed their way off the battlefield to safety, trying with their last breath to save their lives. Women and children walked among the dead as they searched for their loved ones. Clergymen stood over the dead, giving last rites in Latin, praying for their eternal salvation before they met their maker. A battle cry rang across the clearing as he slayed the last man standing, crimson coated his plaid.

Seumas awoke to hissing in his ear and a body thrashing against him. Rolling to his side, he reached for his claymore when he realised it was coming from Serena. Staring at her as she fought an invisible enemy of her own. She withered in pain, curling her lithe body into a tight ball as waves of pain hit her. She gasped for air as she awoke from her torment-induced sleep.

"Serena, my sweet, are ye all right?" he asked as he reached for her.

"Seumas, ye need to get as far away from me as possible. Leave me and bar the door from the outside." She moaned as another wave of pain rushed through her.

"Nay, lass, I will nay leave ye like this. I can help ye." His tone held his desperation.

"Must go, and ye must go now."

"Nay, lass."

"Go, Seumas! I do not wish ye to see me like this. Bar the door."

"Serena, my love, what is happening to ye?" he cried as her eyes closed, praying she could hear his plea.

He prayed to every god, begging him or her not to take her from him. He held her tight against his body, rocking her in his lap. She had told him to bar the door. Why? The why did not matter. The simple fact that she had said to bar the door was enough for him.

Door secured, he turned to the window, opening the curtain, gazing out over the horizon. He watched the changing landscape before him. 'Tis when he noticed movement in the wooded area—two bodies moving against each other. William and Lady Kari, it seemed.

The groans escaping from Serena pulled him free from his thoughts. He went to the bed and scooped her up into his arms, rocking her to ease the pain. Every shiver and muscle contraction she had, he felt it rip its way to the very core of him. He sat for hours until his body ached from the position and demanded he move. Not wanting to leave her just yet, he cared for her body. He poured the water into the basin, his shaft came to life—proof he was going to enjoy caring for her.

Serena's gown was soaked with perspiration. It would be a bitch to get it off her form. He felt his lips curl up in a very devilish smile as he reached for his blade at her waist knowing it would make quick work of removing her gown. The blade cut through the fabric with very little effort, revealing all of her curves to him. He would have a gown brought over and cleaned for her to don.

The pleasure he took from the simple care of her was beyond lust. Seumas took his time patting and rubbing her body dry. Seumas was encouraged by every little mewl she made, renewed his interest tenfold, not that he would ever not want her. His manhood was the only proof he needed. Cradling her in his arms, he carried her to the chair near the window. He stripped the bed of the wet coverings and tossed them aside. He grabbed a new set of linens and quickly remade the bed and placed her in it, making sure she was as comfortable as possible.

"Get rest, my love," he said as he kissed the top of her head. "I must go for now. I will be back," he murmured as he unbarred the door.

He felt a tug of guilt as he barred the door from the outside, as she had requested, instructing his staff not to enter his chamber. He ordered gowns to be brought in from the outer building and cleaned. Satisfied all understood his orders, he sought out William, knowing exactly where to find him. Seumas walked the road to where the campers had pitched their tents. Within moments, William was at his side.

"Forgive me, milord. I meant to join ye beforehand."

"Nay forgiveness required. I know well who occupies yer time. How does Lady Kari fare?"

"Well, she is still having difficulty with her jaw. 'Tis me understanding that Lady Serena found a cure for her discomfort. I'll be at ease once she cures her of her pain. Her discomfort does not sit well with me."

"If Serena says she can help, then she can. It might well have to wait until we find out what these men want from me."

The camp was quiet as they entered. Within seconds, bodies emerged from tents. They watched all gather, waiting for one man. The bodies parted as a nobleman walked forward. He was of average height with thinning hair and a bulge where his stomach should've been. The man's eyes were set deep in their sockets, bitty orbs dull with life, a broad nose, and a thin-set lips hidden under a scraggly beard. It seemed quite fitting that this man and Sir Argyle had been friends. The sound of his voice could've set the dead rolling over in their graves.

"Lord MacIver, thank ye for coming to see me. It saved me time. I am Sir Dougal Reid, and I demand justice for the death of my dearest friend, Sir Argyle."

"Sir Reid, Argyle's death might have been sudden to a very few, but to a great deal more, it was long overdue. The death he received was far quicker than it would've been if he had been brought in front of a magistrate," he said in a tone not hiding his distaste for the subject.

"I shall have justice, MacIver. The bitch who took his life now belongs to me and is mine to kill. The wench dispatched three men, and I will have her life ended," he spat in his apparent rage.

"Ye can nay have her. Seek justice elsewhere," he said, showing his boredom of this conversation.

"Ye bring a war to yer land, MacIver. I grant ye until midday tomorrow to deliver the wench to this camp, or it will be war."

"Do as ye wish, Reid. Ye will not have her. As for Sir Argyle, he got what he deserved. The man was nothing more than a tyrant, murderer of innocent, batterer of women—namely, his wife. Go ahead and push me, sir, for I guarantee ye, I will push back harder," he threatened as he took steps toward this insignificant little man. He towered over this man, which only broadened his smile. "Do not test me, Reid. Ye can nay win this game. Ye have picked the wrong man this time. I will not lie down and roll over for the likes of ye or any man," he growled, unable to keep back the anger he was feeling.

"Ye are going to regret this day, MacIver."

"We shall see who truly will regret this day. I know it will nay be me and mine."

With that said, he turned with William and walked away. Only to find Lady Kari standing feet away with a look on her face indicating she'd heard all.

"Come, lass. 'Tis nothing ye can do. Please do not worry over this," murmured William as he drew her away.

It had been days since she'd received her beating, and she still was unable to move her jaw without causing her extreme pain. The thought of killing Sir Argyle himself crossed his mind often. That had not been his fate. The honour had fallen upon a very mysterious woman.

The fire in the hearth blazed hotter as if it felt the frustration and unmanageable anger in the room. Popping and spitting embers out, sending the small chunks of red-hot wood onto the area rug before it. Seumas watched as the wood burned holes in the rug before he stomped them out and replaced the fire screen. The silence was broken in the room by a soft female voice. It was the first time Seumas heard her speak.

"I can nay let Serena die for me. She could have left me behind and walked out of the keep with no problem, but she did not," she said with a sigh. "I owe her my life, and I would give my life willingly if it shall spare hers," she whispered as tears ran free down her cheeks.

"We saw what she did for ye, lass, and I thank ye for offering yer life in place of hers. I simply can nay allow it."

"There's another way, sweetheart. Ye do nay have to give yer life for hers," he murmured as he rubbed her back.

"Aye, I do. She took care of me after my husband had beat me. He did nay know she was in my chamber. Serena wanted to help me, and I told her nay, so ye see, I owe her." She could feel their gaze on her, and she felt shame hit her hard.

"Serena saw the beating ye received?" asked Seumas with intrigue. "There was a lot of blood, wasn't there?"

"Well, aye."

"Tell me all, lass. What happened, Lady Kari? Do nay leave anything out, nay matter how small a detail," he said, not hiding his curiosity.

Chapter Nineteen

Kari felt for the first time that she held all the answers in the world as she told her story to both men. They gave her their full attention, not interrupting once as she explained how Lady Serena had come to be in her tower chamber. She told them how she had given her hope and how, at first, she'd thought she was sent to dispatch of her. Even telling them, she wanted to die and was ready for it.

" 'Tis enough, lass. I do nay need to hear any more. Thank ye for telling us yer tale. Ye are in a great deal of pain. Please rest now. If I need more information, I shall let William know," he said as he reached for her hand, placing a kiss on her knuckles. "William, take yer woman to rest." Seumas watched as his friend escorted his women out of the study. A great love blossomed between them.

A terrifying roar rumbled through the keep. Serena. Before he knew it, he was square in front of his chamber door. The sound came from within his chamber—more to the point, from Serena. Seumas unbarred the door to his chamber and pushed it open with caution. Seumas stepped inside as quietly as possible and barred the door once again. He scanned the room for Serena. She stood near their bed, her head bowed with nothing covering her form, just as he'd left her. It was a sight he could gaze upon forever.

Her body ached. Her throat felt raw. Her skin was sensitive to the touch, her senses heightened. She stared at her feet, not believing what she saw. On the wood floor lay her microchip. She felt like skipping, jumping, and dancing. Serena was no longer the family pet. They could no longer keep track of her. She was free from being controlled, free to do as she pleased.

"My sweet, are ye all right?" he asked as he walked toward her, love laced in his voice.

Fixated on Serena as she lifted her head to him, he felt himself take in a breath. Her eyes reflected gold in their light-brown depths, eyes that could hypnotise. Lips tinted the colour of cherries. Straight raven-black hair now graced her. Gone were the curls that had framed her face. There was a shimmer upon her skin, and he found himself wanting to run his hands over her newly discovered flesh. Her voice touched his ears, he felt his cock spring to life, and his sac pulled up tight against his body. Almost spilled his seed right where he stood. Her voice was smooth as honey, her scent filled his lungs, and this time, there was no holding back his seed from spilling like an untouched lad.

Serena did not notice Seumas enter the chamber. She was still shocked by her new body. Then, it hit her like a ton of bricks. The natural spice that was him. Her fangs extending, they knew his flesh, knew he would give of himself and she wanted it. His voice brushed her ears, causing a tremor to run through her body. She was hungry, and only he would do. Bringing her gaze to his, she watched as he took in a breath and held it.

"Seumas," she purred as he neared her. Letting her eyes roam over his muscular form in pure delight.

No way she would come across a man like him in modern times. The urge to stay in this time, in this place with him, was overwhelming. At some point, all of this would end, and she'd mourn the loss of it—and more to the point, him.

She felt his touch on her skin, and the feelings rushing through her had her heart beating faster. This was the man she desires most, the man she loved. And she did not want this love to go unnoticed or unspoken. There was no telling when she would be swept back to her time, back to her life in Henderson.

"Seumas, there's much I wish to tell ye about me that ye should know. First, can ye tell me where my gown has gone?" She watched as a very devilish smile crossed his handsome face.

"Ye were in a great deal of pain that yer body's perspiration soaked the delicate silk. So... I cut it from your very lovely body," he said as he ran his hand down her stomach. Her flesh was cooler than before, and he reached for a spare plaid, wrapping it around her before he went to the door.

Sticking his head out, he beckoned his squire. "Have the gowns I have chosen for Lady Serena brought up at once."

"Aye, milord."

"We shall talk about whatever ye wish once ye don a gown. I fear I'm unable to concentrate or maintain any kind of conversation with ye as ye are," he muttered as he regarded her. "Unless ye are willing to talk later. I can think of a few ways to occupy our time," he said with a husky laugh.

She could not help but smile at his cheeky remark. Profoundly touched by the fact that he'd had gowns cleaned for her. Before she knew it, she was kissing him deeply with all the love she felt. Serena was thankful for the knock at the door, announcing her gowns' arrival, she was getting to the point of no return. Laughing softly at the hiss of frustration that crossed his lips, she felt the same, but she had to talk to him.

"Seumas, would ye be so kind as to fetch the gowns? I truly desire to try on what ye selected for me." Wondering about the colours of the gowns and styles that he had chosen for her. Whatever they were, she was going to love them. He had taken time to pick out these gowns for her. Of course she'd be delighted.

"I want nothing more than to watch ye slip into these gowns." The twinkle in his eyes spoke of his cravings. "Mayhap give ye advice on which gowns are most suitable for ye. I am after all somewhat of an expert when it comes to yer figure, lass."

She was not going to justify his remark with a verbal response. She wanted all the help she could get.

Time progressed as he helped her with gown after gown. Caressing and stroking her whenever possible. Leaving a trail of fire blazing within her. He lavished her in the care he took with her, and she wanted it, craved it. Wished this from him for the eternity she would live.

Not one gown did not belong on her body. Not even his wife had looked as well as Serena did at this moment. 'Twas the last gown that graced her body that set his pride bursting free. His colours never looked better than at this very moment. The dark royal blue and black complemented her skin tone. This dress had been made for her; he just had not known it at the time.

Seumas remembered when he had purchased the gown from a dress shop in Edinburgh. The shop and the dressmaker were in high demand, and he had paid a hefty sum for the beautiful dress. It was to be a gift for the birth of their babe. She never got the chance to wear it. He had nay doubt she would have looked lovely in this gown. Serena, however, was exquisite. Much like a porcelain doll made by a master, designed after a goddess with its perfect features.

"I do think this one is my favourite," she purred as she turned to face him. He did not seem to hear her. "Seumas, are ye okay?" she asked, trepidation laced in her voice.

Seumas was engrossed in his thoughts that he did not see her approach him. She gently placed her hand on his forearm, not wanting to scare him out of his mind.

Her gentle touch brought him around.

"My colours suit ye."

Serena felt what he really meant down to the very core of her. His colours, his woman. *Mine*. It thrilled her more than she could say. There was a desperate need deep within her that wanted to be marked by him, marked as his woman for all to see. A silent warning reverberating to all males to fear the grave repercussions, fear what would be done to them if they even attempted to touch what was rightfully his.

The thoughts and the mere sound of his voice softened her a little more. Now was the time to confess all to him. She needed to be brave.

Where to begin and just how far back should she go? She guessed it would be best if she started at the beginning.

"Seumas, love, let's sit by the window and talk," she said with fretfulness in her voice. She only hoped he would hear all she had to tell. "Seumas, what year is this?" she asked, and she saw the confusion on his face, but he answered all the same.

" 'Tis the year 1374, lass."

"Thank you for answering my question. I know ye don't understand, but I hope ye shall as I recount my life history for ye." There was no way for Serena to say this fast, so she had better start now. "I was born in the winter of 1101." She paused for his reaction.

"How can that be? That would make ye over two hundred years old. Ye do nay look any older than two and twenty."

She could not help but smile at his remark, relieved he was still sitting and listening to her and not running from her.

"Seumas, I have already told ye that the blade brought me here, to this time," she said as she pulled the blade from her waist, hoping he could fill her in on how it had done it. "My current century is the twenty-first century. I am over nine hundred years old, and I will never die of old age. Though there are a few ways to kill me that my body cannot regenerate from."

He paled at least three shades. She really couldn't blame him. She would've done the same. He seemed to be in complete shock.

" 'Tis nay possible!"

"Aye, Seumas, it is. I am a vampire. The living dead. Nosferatu. The undead."

That one rang a bell.

"This is why I need blood—for nutrients. I am able to survive on food, but I am weakened by it. With blood, I am always at top strength."

"In what ways can ye be killed?"

"If I lose my head, a silver stake to my heart and the sun. Though I am not sure any more about the sun. My body went through the change this very day. I have lived among humans for so long now that I am not sure if the sun could kill me any longer." She paused for a moment as she pondered on that thought, did the sun still pose a threat to her? "Perhaps a test is in order," she murmured as she flung back the curtain from the window.

Nothing happened. Not even the burning sensation she'd felt in the past.

Turning to face him, only to be tackled to the ground by him, she should've hit the wood floor much harder than she did. He held her close, cushioning her fall. Staying on top of her, shielding her from the sun's reach, breathing in her scent as deeply as possible.

"I've seen ye in full daylight. How is the sun capable of killing ye?" Seumas was desperate to grasp what she was saying to him.

It didn't matter to him—who or what she was. Seumas wanted her even if it meant she would outlive him. He held magic within him. Mayhap he could find an incantation that would give him immortality. Life without her was nonexistent. He had already lost so much, and it was time for him to be happy.

Chapter Twenty

The honesty exhibited by her was beyond moving. He could see she feared what she had divulged to him. The apprehensiveness of the unknown and what he might do radiated off her very being. The intense urge to comfort her swept through him. He knew she had never shared this part of herself with anyone. The admiration and esteem he held for her was in the highest of regards. He did not want her to fear him in any way. The knowledge she had shared with him was the ultimate power over her. In the wrong hands, it would mean her death, yet her death was exactly what Dougal Reid demanded. Mayhap he could use this to his advantage. A perfect opportunity to deceive Reid, pull the wool over his eyes. Utilize the information about his woman, come up with a plan together.

Serena held nothing back from him, no hidden agenda and no games played with his heart. She gave her love boldly and freely, with no hidden trickery to get him to say it first. She gave of herself courageously with honesty and trust he would give her the like in return.

Serena observed Seumas with unwavering eyes as his muscles tensed in his body as he stood. His body was rigid as he pondered over his thoughts. Within seconds, the tight, stiff muscles gave way. Obviously, he came upon a decision about her. She prayed he showed her mercy. She was aware of how he felt about her, but fear still ran wild within her, and her blood turned cold as she waited for him to speak his mind.

"Thank ye for disclosing all, lass." He saw the fear and anticipation in her eyes. "Ye asked me once how I was able to keep pace with ye. I wish to reveal all to ye now," he said with a sigh. "My uncle raised me after my family's death. A plague swept through the village and killed all, except me. I came to be the lord of this keep by way of my uncle after his death. He taught me many things as a lad, magic being one of those things."

He saw the recognition flash in her eyes. As quickly as it had appeared, it disappeared within seconds, leaving only the light dancing upon her eyes.

"That was how ye were able to keep pace with me. Ye tapped into yer power," she said with wonder in her voice. "What else can ye do? Do ye think ye would be able to send me back to my time?" she asked hopefully.

She watched him carefully as his emotions froze him in place before he answered her.

" 'Tis what ye wish, lass—to be sent back to yer time? I fear I could nay do that. I would be cutting out my own heart if I sent ye away. Please, do not ask this of me. I beg of ye."

"Seumas, love, I do not wish to leave ye. These feelings I have for ye are strong. Like none, I have ever felt before for any man, mortal or immortal alike. All I wish is to leave word with my dear friends, the Heffernan to let them know I am safe. Then, I will have the peace of mind to truly be here with ye. Tell me ye understand," she whispered as tears rimmed her lids.

"Do not cry, lass. I will see what I can do to help ye, but I will be going with ye. This is the only way I can let ye go. I have to know ye are safe."

"Oh, thank ye, thank ye, thank ye," she said, throwing herself into his arms.

"Now that we have this settled, shall we continue my tale?" he asked as he looked upon her with a twinkle in his eyes.

The love in his eyes had her heart skipping beats.

"Please, go on," she said, smiling up at him, hoping it would encourage him to go on with his life history.

The next part of his tale he did not want to talk about, not because it caused him pain, but he did not wish to see her reaction to it. How could he nay tell her all? She had given of herself without hesitation. So would he.

"I was once married." The straightforward statement got the reaction he had expected. Yet it was not that of surprise, but one of curiosity. "My marriage was not meant to be. My wife and unborn child were slayed in their sleep. I failed that night as a husband and a father. Their ghosts have been with me for so long—until now," he whispered as he gently rubbed his knuckles down the soft slope of her cheek. "You saved me from the haunting of my soul. From the haunting of my dreams."

Serena felt his thankfulness wash over her. She had finally found the love she had sought for so long. And it had only taken her a little over nine hundred years to find it.

"Now, ye know all, lass. Well, mayhap not all. I have yet to tell ye my plan for Reid. He wishes yer death, or it shall be war I welcome at my door. I will fight until my last breath is taken from me to save ye. I want to use what ye just told me about yerself to fool Reid into thinking ye are dead."

He did not want to contemplate on the torturous death Reid planned for her. Yet it was not the torture that drove fear through his heart. It was the rape of her body that was sure to happen in an attempt to break her willfulness. This man and the men who surrounded him would rape and murder their own mothers if it meant they gained.

The expression frozen on her face told him all he needed to know. She was not going to allow this facade to take place. She was no coward. Not one to hide behind her man and the protection offered by him. The image of her clad in armor, claymore in hand, fangs bared, hissing her fury at an opposing force flooded his mind. She would be a sight to behold. This same hissing brought him back from his thoughts.

"I see ye are not going to go alone with me plan." He felt the frustration start to boil over. Of course, it would not be that easy.

"I won't play this part and put ye in more danger. Reid could go to yer king and demand yer death if he sees through this treachery," she roared at him, not able to help herself, her emotions running wild within her. "Ye won't put yer life at risk in place of mine. I cannot allow it. If ye were to be killed, I would be utterly alone for eternity, and I do not think I could do it again. My life has been one of solitary wandering for the past nine hundred years, and now that I've found ye, I won't let ye put yer life in danger for mine. I love ye with all of my heart," she whispered.

Seumas experienced her emotions as if they were his own. He understood how she felt. He felt the same about her. He had to make her see it his way. Then, he heard the words he'd longed to hear for so long. Those three little words had his heart pounding hard in his chest. The only thought he could hold firm to was his absolute love for her. He would have her as his wife, and as for the matter at hand, they would come up with a new plan. That was the last coherent thought he remembered as he reached for her. Seumas held tight to her as he declared his profound love for her in Gaelic, a language he always thought to be beautifully romantic.

Serena did not fully understand all of what he was saying to her, but it had her feeling all tingly inside. She felt her very bones melt down into her toes, pooling at the very tips of them. She clung to him and his embrace as if her life depended upon the feel of him. The warmth in this caress was everything she had ever wanted, and Reid was putting a threat on this love by asking for her death. She'd stand with him in battle as they fought a common foe.

Their bodies pulling away from each other at the same moment as if they had the same thought, the same needs. Serena hoped that was the case as she tilted her face up to him, a realisation hit her, and it scared her to death. She might not die if injured. Her body would heal, given time. Seumas's body would heal if a minor injury was acquired. If a fatal blow was dealt, game over. His mortality has now been elevated to an obscene obsession in her eyes. This would be her downfall. Turning him was her only option. He would not die and leave her alone. She longed for mortality and the end of her life, which never came. Now that she had found this, she did not wish for death any longer. Instead, she found herself embracing her immortality for the first time in far too long.

They knew they were left with two options. Stand and fight, blade to blade and blood to blood. On the other hand, they could ride hard to the king's court and pray he would hear their plea. The likelihood of that happening was non-existent. The king was known well for his mood swings, and ye never knew what the outcome would be. She had been in this time but a handful of days and heard the villagers talk about the king's erratic mood swings. By the sound of it, he had a mental disorder. The possibility of them being sent to the guillotine was high. There would be no heads rolling this day.

"We shall stand and fight side by side, lass. For I do not wish to take this matter to the king. Yer neck shall not be put to the blade. Nay telling what mood the king might be in once granted an audience," he said as he held her even closer. "Ye must promise me ye shall keep safe and not take any unnecessary risk. Is that understood, lass?"

"I promise ye here and now that I will keep safe, my love."

Before she knew what happened, she found herself pinned to the bed under the weight of her man. He felt so right. This was where he belonged. No man had ever felt this way to her. This was the last coherent thought she had.

Chapter Twenty One

The keep woke to pounding reverberating throughout the halls. The call to arms was shouted as men ran the halls, waking the still-sleeping residents.

Reid had attacked the sleeping keep in hopes of finding them off guard. Apparently, he had grown weary in waiting for him to hand over Serena. He should've expected this treachery from the man. A man who had lost his honour long ago, even still, Reid thought he would win the battle. War was now upon his front door, and Seumas wanted nothing more than to slam this man hard into the ground till there was nothing left of this man.

The day held such promise. It had the potential of being a lovely day. He guessed it would be. Seumas could think of no better way to start his day. His woman by his side as they marched into battle, the faith they have in each other to stay safe. Nay risk taken that put their life in danger. Knowing full well that he would break that promise if it meant sparing her life. He could only hope she forgave him if it came down to that. Seumas knew he would be asking much from her. The world was better with her in it. It would become a very dark, bitter place if she was lost to him forever. He had never realised how alone and dark the world was or how desperate he was for love. She had given him so much without him ever knowing in so little time. He wouldn't give that up without a fight.

The pounding faded as music touched his ears. A tune so mystical that it enchanted the very soul.

Serena had never been this happy. She couldn't remember the last time she had sung so freely and carefree. Never a time she had felt safe or loved before this. Even with war beating down the keep doors, there was still a feeling of safety. Seumas made it secure and sheltered for those he loved. Now, she was part of that select few. He honoured her more than he knew.

"My warrior, I am ready to meet the day and the battle at hand," she murmured as she reached for him.

Together, they stood, and together, they would be victorious.

Walking the corridors leading out of the keep, they felt the tension in the air thicken as they neared the keep door. Tension so thick it was meant to suffocate, to place fear in the heart of those opposing forces. A lesser man would've given in to this fear and crumble. Whimpering like some untrained lad, hiding behind his mother's skirts. You could feel the fear coming from Reid's men as they met the bloody end of a blade, wielded by Seumas's men. The day held defiant promise. It had been so long since he had warred against any clan. He found himself eager to shed blood. To draw first blood and see the fear surface within the depths of their eyes.

"Aye, a very fine day indeed," he said with a broad smile. "Shall we join them in the fight, my sweet?" he said as he kissed her hand.

She needed no further invitation. Fight she would, for his and her lives depended on it. She could not be put to the gallows or the guillotine. The hanging would only piss her off, and the guillotine most certainly would end it all. There would be no more cool breezes, no shadowed skies, and no lush green fields to walk barefoot in. Most definitely no Seumas touching her body as he placed kisses upon her. The losing of one's head did not sit well with any soul.

The war cries rang across the bailey as men charged toward one another, weapons at the ready. Armour and blades clanged as bodies met an opposing force. The smell of blood hung heavy in the air as blades tore through soft, warm flesh. Bodies crumpled to the ground as their lifeblood ran free. Men littered the ground, coating the earth crimson. The moans from the injured and dying echoed through the air, no thought was spared to them as the battle raged on as each side fought for victory.

Seumas scanned the area around him, searching for Serena. A sigh of relief escaped his lips as he saw his goddess still standing. Lust so strong coursed through him at the mere sight of her.

"Time to end this," he called out to his men. "MacIver to me. Wulff! Wulff to me!" Within minutes, his men and women surrounded him. " 'Tis time to end this game Reid is playing."

"As you wish, my warrior."

The fight continued around them as Seumas gave his orders. With the plan now set in motion, they advanced on Reid's numbers. Serena watched in horror as all went in slow motion. She watched, frozen in place, as her warrior was attacked from behind, his back left unguarded as his man moved in to fight the enemy. Her eyes locked with his as he collapsed to the ground, gasping for air. Fear and loss hit her so hard that she felt as if she had hit the hard ground herself. It sent her in a blind rage, attacking Reid's men.

"I cannot lose him, not now that I've finally found him," she cried.

Seconds later, his men ended the fight, leaving Seumas's attacker alive for her or him to deal with.

The fire in her eyes said it all as she spoke in a tone only he could hear. "Do not mistake the fact that you still breathe as mercy. For at this moment, I have none. Be sure ye are drawing yer last breath," she said on a hiss.

"Take the prisoner to the dungeon," she shouted as she raced over to Seumas's side.

"Don't ye dare leave me! Ye'll not die on me. Do ye understand me, my love?" she whispered.

"I will miss ye, my sweet. There is nothing that can be done to save me now. Know I love ye," he said as he choked on his blood.

"Nay, my love. Ye shall live out this night."

Tears rimmed her lids, she fought against the pain in her heart. He would live through this night even if it took every drop of her blood to save him.

"Let's get him back to the keep," she said once her emotions were in check.

She saw their looks of concern and wished she could ease the pain and guilt they felt. Nevertheless, nothing could be done. She could not tell them what she was. Her hands might be tied about her secret, but at the very least, she could save their lord.

Reaching his chamber door, she felt herself take a breath. The colour of his skin gave her reason to worry. Seumas is on his deathbed, and Serena knows fast action is needed if she is going to save him. She rushed all out of the room as quickly as she could. She needed to be with him alone.

"Seumas," she murmured. "Please open yer eyes. Open yer eyes, love."

She waited for him to respond. Hope filled her as she saw the fire in his gaze. There was still life within him.

"Seumas, are ye ready to die?" she asked straight out.

No time to waste, beating around the bush. She needed to give him the option before she took his mortality from him.

"Nay, not ready. Want more? Want more of ye," was all he said before falling silent once more.

"My love, listen to me and listen very carefully to what I offer ye. I can save ye. If ye so wish it, I can change ye. Turn ye into what I am—vampire. If, however, ye do wish this, I promise ye a very long life with me," she said with hope in her voice. Hope that she knew she had no right to feel. She knew what the cost would be.

He held her gaze. "I choose ye. Want ye forever. I welcome and accept yer offer," he said as he reached for her. "Love ye, my sweet."

"So it shall be, for I love ye too," she whispered in his ear. "May yer god forgive me for what I do to ye now. For ye shall never be one of his angels. Never to grace his army of souls again."

The warmth in his body was gone, and the cold of the dead was setting in fast.

"Forgive me. I will see ye soon. Please be strong; this might hurt some."

The excitement of turning Seumas had her body humming with delight. Soon, he would be hers forever. All she needed do was drink him dry which would not take her long at this point and an exchange of her blood was required and it would be done. With that in her mind, she thought no more.

A gasp escaped him as the points of her fangs closed down. Even now, with death beating down his door, eager to claim its prize he still held on to his strength. His blood still held the essence of him, and death wanted it. The dark angel already had its claws in him, and it demanded more. Thanks to death, it did not take much to drain him. She felt his heart slow. He was close now. His heart already skipping beats. Within seconds, it would stop, and he would cease to exist. Releasing him, she quickly bit into her forearm, drawing her ancient plasma to the surface. Blood flowed from her, spilling into his open wound. Her blood filled his mouth, and still, he didn't react.

"Seumas, my love. Ye must drink. Ye must drink now," she said as she caressed his cheek.

He wanted to answer her, to let her know he understood. No energy to do so. It took what little strength he had left to swallow what she offered. He found the thought of consuming her blood did not cause him to be repulsed. Quite the opposite, he wanted more. He felt alive, more alive than he had ever felt. Every part of him pulsated, desperate to fly all at once in every direction.

Serena watched in amazement as her warrior's body began to waken once more. In all of her nine hundred–odd years, she never changed a mortal soul. At first, there was no one she wished to have. Then, she did not desire to bestow immortality upon an unworthy human. Even with Seumas being her first transformation, she knew all the stages he would go through. The high. A high that would occur after ye did hella good drugs. The low. Just like any good high, a low would follow along with pain and misery. The pain. Pain so considerable that it silenced yer screams and twisted yer spine as it flowed like lava through yer veins. Deforming the body, driving ye to the black pit of unconsciousness. The only upside was he would not remember any of it.

His body was injured and weak from blood loss, yet he still held power within him. Magic kept him alive, and he had to tap into it. Use what was naturally within him.

Time crept by as she witnessed the intense swings of the stages. She felt each one of them to the very core of her being. The high had him wanting to pin her to the bed and ride her hard. She fought him to keep her clothes on. With every move of his hand, he tried to remove her gown. Before she knew it, the low hit, and it hit hard. However, the pain caused her to regret her action. That, too, passed, and so did her guilt as he slid into the grasp of unconsciousness.

Once he came through, his hunger would be out of control. Blood would be needed to feed him. The first to be served up—the coward in the dungeon. Seumas would deliver his death sentence, and a brutal death it would be.

Chapter Twenty Two

Not until Seumas went lax did Serena realise her mistake. He should've died. The injury he had sustained was a death blow, meant to kill swiftly. What could be done to make this right? She wouldn't be unable to hide from this. It was done. How was she going to explain this to his kinsmen? He would live, and his kinsmen would look differently upon him. Thought of as witchery, as some kind of sorcery. To be looked at as if he had made a deal with the devil himself. To be pushed out as an outcast, never to be heard from again. One thing could save them both, and she prayed they would listen. Take heed with open hearts and minds as she explained to them what she was. She might meet the guillotine yet. That did not matter. Only her warrior mattered now. It was for him that she would do this. She was going to need help.

She thought of going to Kari's chamber in search of her, but she knew better. She had to find William. Serena took comfort in the knowledge that Lady Kari was held in the arms of William each night. She deserved happiness after all the pain and sorrow dealt to her. It took a strong person to live and not wish for death to take her every night. Now, she was going to have to ask for her assistance, putting her in more danger.

With a sigh of regret, she left Seumas's side. Stepping out of the room, she was unable to move no more than two feet before she had to stop. His kinsmen and clansmen alike surrounded his door. Shit, not good. Serena required more time. She had to find William and Kari. With that thought running through her mind, they appeared.

The coward parted as they made their way to her. She had to say something to them all.

"He still lives for now. Please, make room for William and Lady Kari," she said as calmly as she could.

William saw the worry in Lady Serena's eyes. He feared his friend was dead or close to it. Not wishing to ponder that thought, he turned his hopes toward life.

"Milady, I have brought Lady Kari to aid ye," he said with far too much emotion in his voice.

"I welcome both of yer help. Please, come in," she said as she pushed open the door. Once behind the closed door, she felt the uneasiness radiating off them both. "Be at ease, my friends. Seumas is not dead. He but sleeps. I have saved him from death. A death that was certain. This was what I have need to speak to you both about," she murmured. Mustering her strength and faith.

"Say what ye must, milady." William saw the hesitation in her eyes.

"I have to explain and show ye something," she said, taking in a deep breath. "Seumas shall wake, and when he does, he will require blood. Blood to be given without question, without hesitation. His injury was meant to kill. He asked me to save him, so I did—the only way I knew how. I changed him. Transformed him. He's no longer mortal. No longer subject to human illness or death. He is and forever will be immortal. Do ye understand what I am telling ye?" she asked.

Nothing. No response. Just silence. She had to show them—or more to the point, him. On a silent command, her body transformed. She expected a look of horror, of shock. Something other than what she got.

"Milady, nothing ye could say or do would change ye—a kind, caring woman. A woman who saved the life of two people I care for very deeply. I should be the one thanking ye for all ye've done," he said as he bowed to her.

For the first time in her very long life, she felt she truly had a family. All that was missing was Kimmie, Tommy.

Maybe that could be fixed too. If Seumas found a way to return them to her time, he could find a way to bring Kimmie and Tommy back to his time. To be able to bring up their children in mediaeval Scotland. Yet still have the convenience of modern medicine when required. To be able to go back and forth between times. To live life in a simpler time, a simpler place.

Hope flared to life within her. How she would love that life. The family she never had, all in the same place, in a time that was more vibrant and alive. A time and place where people knew how to truly live and love.

William's acceptance of her meant more than she had realised. She needed the serenity his acceptance brought her and the hope that it brought. Soon, Seumas would be joining her in immortality. No longer would he be part of their world, but part of hers and all that it implied.

Their worlds were day and night, light and dark. Their worlds were always near, always dancing on the edge of one another, but never should the two meet.

A world that he would soon be thrust into. And like a newborn infant, he'd rediscover the world in all its glory. Colours are more vibrant, sight is sharpened. Smells heightened, touch more sensitive. Taste—oh, the taste… taste meant to detect every note every hint of flavour. The senses are awakened by the creature of the night.

He'd awaken in his new body with new abilities to boot. And still, the fear within her stirred to life. Not fear for her, but fear for him. He was going to be reborn as a vampire, and along with it all the needs and desires that came with it.

"Do ye truly understand, William, what yer lord shall become?"

"Ladyship, ye have not to worry about. Milady told me all about ye," he said, trying to ease her worries. A smile warmed his face as he saw Serena relax.

Deciding to change the subject from Seumas, William thought it best to thank Serena for the pain relief she had given to his Kari.

"Milady, I wanted to thank ye for what ye did for milady," he said as he pulled Kari close.

"William, I do wish ye would call me Serena. I am yer friend, and friends call each other by their given names."

She hoped he would not think her too forward in this statement. Knowing well that one did not call ye by yer given name if one just met ye.

They seemed to settle in around the fire, talking about whatever crossed their minds. Laughter and love filled the room around them. They tried desperately to lighten the mood in the room as the eleventh hour approached. Even with the lightness in the air surrounding them, there still seemed to be uneasiness about them. Time went on. They all seemed to be looking over toward Seumas more and more. Serena could feel their uncertainty as time marched on. She wished she could reassure them, yet she could not.

Then, she felt it. The connection between her and Seumas flared to life. She knew he would be waking soon and hunger along with it. A hunger she would be happy to feed. She turned back to her friends; it was time for them to leave and fetch the prisoner. Not wanting them around when he first awakened, she could not guarantee their safety, at least not at first.

"What is it, Serena?" asked Kari with more than a little curiosity laced in her voice.

"Time for ye both to leave. He shall be waking at any moment. Go and bring up the prisoner. But do not enter until ye are granted entrance, understood?" she asked, making sure they did as she had instructed. "I'm not sure how he is going to wake. I will be able to control him better if I do not have to worry about the both of ye." Serena sent up a silent prayer to what gods she might still believe in.

"We understand, Serena. Do nay distress yerself. We'll do as ye bid," said William as he escorted Kari from the chamber.

"Thank ye both. I don't think I would've been able to do this by myself," she said as she rushed over to their side, feeling the need to hug them both at once. "It has never been easy for me to ask for help. But with friends like ye, I see myself trusting and relying on ye without worry. Thank ye."

"Ye are nay longer alone in this world, Serena. Ye have us now. We shall be yer family and friends," William said as he hugged her one last time before departing the chamber.

He could see why Seumas loved her. A very pure soul lay within her.

Taking a deep breath, she barred the door shut. Not wanting to take the chance that he would push his way through. Even though she knew that would be physically impossible. Her blood was in him, and his blood would recognize hers and yield to the greater power.

For now, her concern centred on the safety of his kinsmen and clansmen alike. She did not want him to regret anything. There would be no remorse for him. He'd start his new life with her at his side for all eternity, and she could not ask for anything better.

She'd be there to help him through his time of transition. Help ease him into his new lifestyle. A lifestyle change that would take him some time to get used to. Time was one thing she had on her side. It was all she ever truly had on her side. Now, time did not look so grim. Hell, her future seemed to be going more to the bright side of things. Fate has finally shined down upon her, and it was a warmth she could bathe in, the warmth of her man.

Chapter Twenty Three

Serena sat on the edge of the bed gazing down at Seumas, running her hand down the angry red scar, which now graced his flawless chest. She knew all too well that angry red scar would soon be gone and, in its place, perfect, unmarred, tanned flesh. Proof that his body truly was one of her kind. Even his skin felt cooler to the touch. His shoulders a little broader, his muscles a littler leaner, changes ever so slight that the human eye would not perceive. Yet to her, these differences were as noticeable as the fangs in her mouth.

The mere thought of fangs got her hot. She could almost feel the points of his fangs rubbing against her sensitive flesh. Experience the pressure of them as they sank deep into her neck. Feeding him her life force as he penetrated her body. This was what she had been waiting for, for so long. He was the reason she stopped having an interest in immortal males. Her mind, heart, and body had been awaiting him. All this time, she had known he was out there. She had no idea she would have to go back in time to find him, to a past she had already lived long ago.

Now that she had him, she was not letting go without a fight. She would fight for him against all odds, protecting him against all enemies was all that mattered. He was her life now.

How had she fallen for this man so quickly? There lay the mystery. Her subconscious had known he would be coming into her life.

The fog lifted from his mind. His body finally awakened from its slumber. Freeing him from his sleep-induced snare. Slowly, he felt sensations come to life throughout his body. Seumas was desperate to cling to these feelings. It was his own dark, erotic heaven, which had him wanting more of what was offered.

The voice he wanted to hear for the rest of his life caressed his ears. What was she saying? That did not matter. The only thing that mattered was her, her touch and scent. He yearned for nothing more than to be engulfed completely by her essence. To be her sexual slave, be her whatever, to be whatever she needed him to be.

Willing his eyes open, Seumas found his woman sitting by his side. Her hand perched gently upon his chest, where the blade ran him through. The hole that should have been in his chest was gone, flesh anew, now replaced the gouge. She had saved him in more ways than one. He would never be able to repay her for the love and kindness she had gifted him. Though he had an idea of how he would like to start. With that thought in his head, his body came fully awake.

Eyes opened, he found himself gazing into the most beautiful eyes he had ever seen. These were the eyes he would regard for all eternity. He found his gaze moving slowly down her face, settling on her full lips. The growl that passed his lips stirred something fierce within him. He wanted her, and he wanted her now. He did not want to wait, and he would not. He grabbed hold of her, intending to kiss her. Within a heartbeat, his need changed. Changed in a way he could not explain.

Serena felt everything her warrior felt, and she knew what he now craved. Bloodthirst had taken over, a thirst demanding to be answered now. Compelled to seal the bond between them by her blood. Her blood would be the first to pass his lips, a first to be taken and in doing so it would ensure he understood how he was meant to feed. She wanted him to take care of the ones he chose to feed off. She did not desire him to kill those he drank from. Yet there was a time and place for taking one's enemies without mercy, to make certain death followed slowly and painfully.

"My love, I know what ye require, and it is not of the sexual kind. Ye must feed, and feed ye shall," she murmured as she moved her hair aside, exposing her neck. "Please, milord, eat. Drink of me and seal the bond that flares between us," she said as she dragged the blade's edge over her exposed column.

Not needing further encouragement, he reached for her, pulled her close to his body, desperate to feel her feminine form pressed against him. It was more than bloodthirst he demanded, the need to feel her sheath tighten around his hard shaft road his hard. To all that was holy, he would have both.

Holding her close, he brushed his mouth over her delicate skin. A tremble went through her, heightened his desire. Then, he felt them—fangs, which felt dark and erotic to him. Dragging his tongue down the length of them testing the sharpness, it was strange and exciting, all at the same time. With all his body was feeling, his cock grew harder. He yearned for his woman in more ways than one.

Seumas pulled the hem of her gown up her long-toned legs making sure his fingertips glided over her sensitive flesh, desperate to feel her engulf him. He thanked the heavens she was dripping for him. He did not think he could hold back his emotions enough to be gentle with her. The next minute, he found himself thrusting deep inside her, pounding his way to release.

Somewhere in the back of his mind, he registered her moaning. The sounds she made set fire running through him. Then, he tasted it—her blood in his mouth—and he wanted more. He could not get enough of her. The mere thought of possessing her in such a way sent him climaxing. His orgasm was hard and fast; the roar that ripped from his throat rumbled off the walls.

As his haze cleared, something else filled his senses. He was drawn to the sounds and smells just beyond the chamber door. Hissing in his frustration, unable to move. Almost at the door, yet still so far away. He was not able to move any further. Seumas looked down at his chest to see a small feminine hand resting upon his chest, she held him back with but a hand.

"I know what ye sense, my warrior. And I can't allow ye to harm yer kinsmen and clansmen alike. The bloodthirst is riding ye hard, and very soon, blood shall be brought to ye," she said, hoping to make him understand. "I am having William and Kari bring up the man who tried to kill ye. I had him placed in the dungeon. Ye may dispatch of him as ye wish," she said as a tear slipped down her cheek.

The knock at the door grabbed both of their attention. Seumas reacted to the noise as any new vampire would. Every sound he heard was heightened, every taste more pure, each and every smell was more vivid than the last. She had to back him away from the door. Serena did not desire to risk the chance he might bolt out of the door.

"My warrior, back away from the door." She waited for him to do as he had been told, and nothing. "DO IT! NOW!"

That got the response she'd demanded.

His eyes drifted down to hers. The love and the concern held in her eyes for him touched him more than the urge running wild within him. He stepped back from the door with a hiss on his lips, Seumas did not like the fact that he had to move, yet, moving served a purpose. Soon, the coward who had stabbed him in the back would be trapped in the room with him. The mere thought that he would soon have his hands on the man had him buzzing on a high, he wanted to drive fear deep into the heart of the coward before he took his life. Seumas wanted nothing more than to let fear and terror strike to the very core, to paralyse with fear, before he attacked.

The ability to extract the punishment elevated his desire to kill. The sensation he felt was new to him in many ways, but never had he felt this way before, not even when his wife and unborn child had been taken from him. The thought of losing Serena caused his heart to turn cold as a Highland winter.

Pupils dilated as the door to the chamber opened. The smells that hit him knocked him back on his heels. He was now able to pick out each of his family and friends by their scent. His heart grew larger with the knowledge that they gathered outside his chamber door out of true concern for him.

It was the man who now entered his chamber that demanded his attention. Trepidation radiated from his eyes. Tension strung his body tight. Measured footsteps took him forward to meet his end. A fate he'd brought upon himself. The coward's voice cracked as he spoke to Serena his eyes focused only on her, he did not seem to notice Seumas, this man was a coward begging for his life.

"I told ye, sir, these are the last breaths ye would be taking," she said, stepping closer to him, baring her fangs. "I do hope ye made yer peace with God. I see ye did not. For ye did not think I meant what I said," she said, leaning in even closer to his ear. "I assure ye, ye won't be walking out of this room alive. Ye sealed yer fate the moment ye attacked milord from behind. So, there shall be no mercy for ye," she whispered as she turned to her man.

Serena knew he followed her gaze. She felt his heart rate quicken, and the smell of fear filled the room around them.

"Come, my love," she murmured as she held out her hand.

Seumas moved to his woman with grace and ease that came with the predator within. She'd thought him a god before, when he was but a mere mortal man. Now, with her bloodline running in his veins, he truly was a god among man, her dark, erotic vengeful god, forever.

Her attention brought back to reality by the sounds being made from the terrified man next to her. The noises the man was making brought back memories of her past wrongs she made against the human race. She still couldn't find mercy for this man. He had almost succeeded in the taking of Seumas's life. She wouldn't be the one to grant mercy if mercy was given. That was for Seumas to decide and no other.

Chapter Twenty Four

Seumas relished in the complete and utter terror coming off of the man in waves that now stood just behind his soon-to-be bride. He loved the sound of the word *bride*. Aye, he would have Serena as his wife. Right now, he craved nothing more for this man to know the end was near. The taste of dread coated his tongue and filled his lungs. The taste and smell in some small way gave him satisfaction, but it was nay enough. He was going to drain this man dry of his lifeblood.

Seumas took Serena's delicate hand she had offered him, placing a soft kiss upon her knuckles. Smiling gently at her, he lifted his head. The warmth and the softness faded as he turned to face his enemy. It was at that exact moment the man fled to the door, trying desperately to escape. Seumas stood at the door before the man even realised what happened.

Grabbing hold of him, he threw him across the chamber with but a flick of his wrist. Seumas watched in satisfaction as the coward slammed hard against the stone wall, his body slumped on the floor.

Even with the pain that must be radiating through him, he still tried to get away. This man did not know when to play dead, Seumas stalked the ground between them consuming the distance between them, becoming the predator that would soon become natural to him. He felt power, strength and grace with each step he took. Liking the way it made him feel. Even with all going on within him, he still felt like himself. More to the point, he felt alive.

He reached for the man that now crawled on all fours, attempting to stand. His body was still not capable of that feat as the pain still lingered, not yet healed from the damage it had sustained. Seumas wanted to be done with this. He had better things to do—namely, his woman. He would have her as his bride and heavy with his seed very soon. First, he was going to dispatch himself of this man.

He felt the man struggle under his hold and tired of it. Time to end it. Seumas turned his attention back to this scum of a man. "Ye ready to meet yer maker?" he asked as his fangs extended to their fullest extent.

"What kind of evil are ye?"

"I am the one that's going to end yer life. This shall be the last day ye are ever to see," he said with more than a little gratification.

He gave no warning as sharp points pushed through leathery, tanned flesh. Blood filled his mouth, holding fear and hatred within it. Those notes were only a hint of what the blood offered. To Seumas, this man was an untapped bottle of wine. One which had been uncorked and needed to breathe, allowing the robust flavours to reach their fullest potential, but that was not possible, this man's life will end tonight.

As he drank from the man struggling in his grasp, he felt him go lax. His body gave up the fight as its life force faded to a dull beacon. Heart rate slowed as it lost the fight for survival. His body realised death was upon it. Then, it happened. Seumas sensed the exact moment the heart stopped and the man ceased to exist.

Even with the knowledge that he caused his death, he still experienced an overwhelming joy. There would not be any more troubles headed Serena's way. They would be able to live their lives with each other without having to look over their shoulders for danger.

Letting the limp form drop to the floor, he moved back to Serena and tugged her into his arms, engulfing her in his love. Holding her tightly to him, he thanked the heavens for keeping her safe and out of harm's way. Even the knowledge of her capability of taking care of herself did little to ease his nerves. She could have been attacked after they ran him through.

That was all behind them now. Time for new beginnings. He shed his mortal body and soul. To be reborn into his new immortal life. He didn't regret his choice, his forever just beginning.

"Seumas, my love. There's much for us to discuss."

"Aye, love, now, we have all of eternity to talk about whatever we wish." He knew exactly what he wished to confer with her about, and it did not include talking unless it involved her moaning under him.

"My warrior, we need to figure out what is to be said to yer people. We have to explain ye still being alive. You and I both know, as does everyone else, ye should be dead," she said on a sigh. "I stopped the natural order of things for my own selfish needs. I could not lose ye. Not so soon," she murmured as her tears slipped quietly down her cheeks.

"Do nay cry, sweetling. Together, we shall explain to my kinsmen and clansmen alike. Nay need for yer tears. Ye have done only what I asked of ye. I was not ready to die. For I feel the same as ye. I have not had enough time with you. I am beginning to think that forever is the only thing I will accept. 'Tis because of ye that we shall have forever. 'Tis only because of ye," he said as he gently tilted her chin up to him, intending to kiss her.

Their lips touched softly at first. Gently exploring one another and the tenderness they shared. He knew she wished for more. He sensed it, and he would give her what she wanted, what she so desperately desired.

Serena found herself pinned up against the bedpost and her warrior's hard body and the mere forcefulness of it had her body dripping for him. She was unable to help herself. He kissed her, and all she desired was him deep inside of her. Before she knew it, she sent her silent request to him. She did not think he would receive it. He had just turned, and from what she understood, new vamps needed to be trained, skills had to be honed. Seumas was proving to be the exception in this case.

"I will have yer full attention, mistress," he murmured. Pulling her from her thoughts.

"Yes, my warrior. Oh… God, yes," she panted as he ran sharp points over her soft, tender flesh.

Her hands tangled themselves in his tartan, needing the support his body offered. Her body quivered in delight as a fire burned at every place Seumas touched.

The soft whimpers coming from her drove him more, he wanted her to scream his name. He demanded her complete surrender. Her body moved against his in such a seductive, inviting way. All he yearned for was to touch, lick, and nip her exquisite body. To mark her as his, to have her body beg for his and all the pleasure he could bring. To have her body remember what he offered from the briefest of touches.

"Milord, milady, are ye all right?" cried William from behind the barred door. Not able to hide the sense of urgency in his voice.

He still held fear in his heart for his friend, and he was unable to shake the feeling. William rapped on the chamber door once again, beyond desperate to get in. He had to see for himself that Seumas lived. That he truly lived and he had not imagined the movement he had seen.

"Milady! Prithee, Serena, let me in!"

William's pleas ripped Serena out of her dark sexual haze. It was the dismay in his tone that did it. She understood that apprehension he felt for a dear one. Finding the strength deep within her, she silently willed her warrior to stop. She couldn't allow them to torment his clansmen and kinsmen alike out of their own selfish needs. They would have all of eternity to scratch that itch. For now, they had to address all. Let them see he still lived and all was well.

With a hiss upon his lips, he stopped the attention he had been giving. He wanted to be deep inside her, pounding their way to ecstasy, yet he stopped. Withdrawing from her body, he smoothed out her gown. A growl rumbled up from deep inside him as he gazed into her eyes. He saw the need, the desire within them. There was no doubt that she was ready for him.

"What is it, lass?" he murmured with a little too much frustration laced in his voice. All he could see was their bodies joined and her panting his name as he pleasured her. Closing his eyes, he pictured only that.

Serena watched in fascination at a very controlled new vampire. She had expected to have to peel him off of her. To have some kind of fight on her hands. This had to be the work of his magic. So far, he had complied with every command. Even still with him yielding to her every command, there was quite a lot to teach him. Teach him she shall.

Before she could answer him, the pounding on the door started once again. And the desperation in William's voice cut through Seumas's haze. The pain that was being caused to William by not knowing if he lived or died, Seumas was unable to withstand it.

"Open the door, lass," he murmured.

Serena moved to do his bidding. She would have not let him near the chamber door anyway. Too much temptation behind the door. At the same time, she did not want to let William and Kari in. Not wishing to put them both at risk. Serena knew she was going to have to be on the watch for any hint of change within her warrior. Though he might prove her wrong. Praying that was the case, she couldn't help but smile her approval as Seumas moved to the far side of the chamber.

Chapter Twenty Five

William still was not too sure if his laird would live to see the next dusk. Time had gone by, and still, he had not heard a word from them. Straining his ears to pick up some form of noise behind the door that barred him from the chamber. Yet there was none. His control snapped. He needed proof of life. So many things could've gone wrong in the time it took for him to reach the dungeon and his lord's chamber. Rapping on the door, as instructed, once the prisoner was brought up. He had intended to go inside, but his new mistress had other plans.

William felt himself take a breath as he entered the chamber, scared of what he might find. The room was sparsely lit with candles. Smothered flames in the hearth took the place of a roaring fire that had blazed just moments before. Curtains drawn. Darkening the room further. He scanned the chamber, searching for his friend. Expecting to find him on the bed. Nothing! He was not found on the bed. Instead, he stepped out of the shadows.

A sigh of relief crossed his lips as he saw his friend and lord step out into the open, alive and well. Serena had done it. She had saved him. He knew at this moment he'd held doubt within his heart if she could do what she said.

Wanting nothing more than to believe in all she told him, desperate to know how she did it. Serena had delivered a miracle.

Serena watched William and Seumas closely. A split second before her warrior bit into William's flesh, she tapped into his mind. Taking the hunger into herself. Knowing full well that if she did not, he would kill his friend with no remorse, and what he had done wouldn't hit him until the bloodlust faded. It was more than that.

"Seumas," William whispered, his tone holding back the emotions he felt. "Ye are truly well." This time William was unable to hold back what he felt.

Reaching out, he grabbed him in a tight embrace, needing to make sure he was real. A warning alarming went off in William's head the moment he touched him. He had known he would come back different. Yet he was not sure what that meant. He knew now. There was a great new power within him. The warning now stronger than ever, he pulled away.

"William, I need ye to back away from Seumas. Do it very slowly. Back away. Follow the sound of my voice, but do not turn around to face me," she said in a very calm voice. "Go ahead, William. Do as I have instructed."

Serena watched in satisfaction as he obeyed her command at once. Once he reached her side, she moved in front of him before she addressed her warrior.

"Seumas, I know what ye want. I see it within yer eyes. Ye must learn to control it. It will take some time, but ye will be able to coexist with humans once more," she murmured as she walked toward him. "Look at me, my love. Look at me. See me. That's it. Now, I want ye to focus on yer magic. Come on, baby. Focus. Ye can do this," she said as she turned his face toward hers. "Ye can do this. Dig deep and pull yer magic forth. There ye go. Ye feel the power, don't ye?" she asked in a soft voice.

He nodded his reply.

"That's good. Now, pull yer magic and wrap it around yer bloodthirst. Pull it tight around the bloodthirst. Do ye have it?" she asked. Knowing full well that he did.

"Aye, sweetling, I feel the control. Still want more blood though," he said as his eyes moved to the door.

"I know ye do, and ye shall have it," she said as she turned to William. "William, we need to come up with an explanation for all those who await an answer."

"Get him back in bed. They need to think he is wounded and needs time to heal. Wrap bandages around the wound and then soak the area with blood. We need to make it look as real as possible," said William as he turned to face the hearth. "I know what ye fear, Serena. I fear the same. We are not going to mention this to anyone else. At least, not until he has healed—or I should say when he would have healed if he was mortal," he said with a smile.

He turned back to Seumas. "Milord, ye wish for more blood. I now offer ye mine," he said as he moved forward.

William watched as his lord turned to face his lady. With a nod of her head, he moved toward him.

Serena wanted to show him that he could take what was needed in a gentle way. To be more humane in taking, a chance to be better than she ever was.

"Thank ye, my friend," he said as he lifted his wrist to his mouth. "I will not take much, just enough to ease the cravings."

"Take what ye need, my friend," he said as he placed his hand on his shoulder, intending to ease his fears.

He stood still, awaiting the bite and the pain that was sure to come. Nothing. He felt nothing, no pain. Just the slight tug on his flesh as Seumas fed. He should've been repulsed by this, yet he was not. Instead, in its place, was honour. Privileged by the fact he was trusted enough to hold this secret safe. Then, it was over. The tugging stopped.

"Thank ye, my friend," murmured Seumas as he sealed William's wounds.

His hunger was now under control, and he knew the hunger in his eyes would be gone as well. It did not take much blood to satisfy him. Knowing full well it was due to his magic and Serena. For now, he was able to face his dear friend without wishing to drain him dry of his precious lifeblood. He had to master his hunger and quickly.

"Time, my friend, to put yer plan into motion," he said as he looked over to his lady. "Go and ready the clan, William, as it will give us time to put bandages on."

Seumas moved away from his friend and toward Serena with more vitality than he should have at the moment. He needed to look sickly—more to the point as if death had knocked on his door.

"Come, sweetling. Time for ye to take me to bed," he said with a smile.

Serena knew what he yearned for, and she desired nothing more than to give it to him. Now was not the time. He would have to wait. Then again, no harm in rubbing her body up against him, heating his blood. She intended to have him so heated that his clan would truly think him wounded.

Seumas saw the excitement flash in her eyes but quickly disappeared. Replaced by calmness—nay, not calmness, something more carnal, more predatory, and still all her. His body demanded whatever she offered him. He knew full well that if she asked for his immortal life, he would give it without question, he would always give her whatever she wanted.

Following her as she led him over to his bed, he gazed at her hips as they swayed hypnotised by their movement.

"Come, my warrior. Sit," she purred. "I want ye to sit right there and do not move or touch me. Is that understood?" she asked as she let her hair down. Getting the response she was looking for at once from her warrior. "That's my good boy. All I want ye to do is watch and resist the urge to touch me. This is just for ye," she said as she placed a kiss upon his roughened cheek.

Serena recalled all those times she had visited strip clubs prowling for prey as she pulled a song from her memory, one that was fit for a lap dance. Only one song came to mind. She had to smile, for it was always the same song playing when she visited a gentlemen's club. Few and far between as it might have been, but it was always the same song playing in the background. Poison had to have made a bundle off the song "Sweet Cherry Pie."

Her body moved to the beat in her mind as she teased him. Rubbing her body against his. Stripping out of her gown as she did so. His erection was plain to see, she straddled him, grinding her bottom against his hard shaft. Felt his every spasm as it tore through his body. Pushing off of him she turned in front of him and dropped into the splits twerking her ass for him. Her ass jiggled in his sight as she continued to twerk as she pulled her knees together getting in a squatting position to give him the full effect.

Seumas groaned deep in his throat as he watched in awe of his woman. She moved in a way that had him hot in seconds. Driving him mad with desire. It took all his strength to do as she had commanded. He wanted nothing more than to grab her and push her down on his mattress to ravish her body. He felt as if someone lit a blazing fire under his flesh. She was so close that he could smell her sex and the moist heat that was offered. With that thought, he came over and over again. He never knew that a woman could use her body in that way to pleasure a man without him entering her body.

"That's it, my warrior," she purred as she leaned against his heated flesh. "Did ye enjoy that? Ye do not have to answer me. I know ye did," she whispered as she turned to face him.

A smile gracing her face, showing her pure satisfaction, she knew damn well what she had done to him. His features tight with control, his skin flush and fire hot to the touch. Oh, yes, she had done her job well. She moved on his lap, and a moan ripped from him. His strong hands wrapped around her upper arms, holding her in place. Not allowing her freedom to move.

"Do nay move," he growled in her ear. "Nay yet."

"Seumas, my love, I need to bandage ye now. William will be upon us at any moment with all in tow. Ye must have bandages on."

She felt his reluctance, but he released her all the same. She moved so fast; he barely had time to miss her.

"Will I be able to move as fast as ye?" he asked with amazement in his voice.

"Yes, with time. Ye shall be faster than any mortal alive. Yer body will heal at a rapid speed—a pace all will notice. Yer sight will be heightened as well as yer hearing. Yer strength will be a hundred times more powerful than any mortal man," she said with reverence. "With yer new abilities comes great responsibility. Because ye are more powerful than any mortal, this does not mean ye can take all that ye want. I will spare ye this horror. This is why we have to take care of all we do. There is much to teach ye. Enough of this conversation for now. I need to finish with the bandage," she said as she stepped back to survey her handiwork.

Before he realised what she meant to do, she slit her wrist. Blood flowed freely from the soft flesh. Running down the sides of her arm, dripping to the ground. Pushing him back down onto his bed with her good arm, gaining better access to his now-wrapped chest. He watched as the blood stained the fabric. Watching as her blood ran free and stained the material that now covered his chest. Seumas had to endure watching as she slit her wrist several more times before she was satisfied with the results.

Taking her wrist in his hand once she finished, he examined the angry red marks that now graced her delicate milky-white shin. Kissing her hand, he tugged her down for a more meaningful embrace. His blood reheating the moment he tasted her delicate flesh. A growl rumbled up his throat as a knock interrupted their kiss. He did not realise his hand had made its way up her thigh. How could it not? She still had yet to dress. He found it very, very hard to concentrate on anything she said. Somehow, he managed to take it all in.

"I must dress and quickly, before William enters," she said as she gathered her things.

"Aye, ye must," he purred as his gaze roamed over her body from his sickbed.

Chapter Twenty Six

Seumas watched his woman dress and pull her hair back. Studying her as she made her way to the chamber door, she reached for the handle, and her hand froze, poised on the handle like she was having second thoughts. Her eyes closed as if saying a silent prayer, he wondered what she could be thinking about. It was a split second in time, but he saw it all the same, then the door opened wide. And a wave of people came rushing through.

He heard her without her even speaking.

"Do not move too much. Ye need to act and move as if ye were wounded. Do not let them get too close to ye. We cannot afford any to suspect something's amiss. Love ye."

Then, her sweet, honeyed voice was gone, and so was she as the many filled his chamber.

Seumas never truly understood how loved he was by his people until this very moment. As each and every one came up to his bed, he learned their smells and the rhythm of their hearts. Learning the heartbeat of each and every one of his clan. Knowing he would be able to find them by their scent alone, no matter where they went.

Awareness hit him. He would witness his friends and family die. How could he explain the fact that he was not aging as others did? Was he going to age at all? If so, how fast or slow would it happen? Would he fake his own death? He would talk to Serena about this. There had to be something they could do. There had to be. How had she lived this long without one?

Serena felt his distress and wished she could remedy it. Yet nothing could be done for him at the moment. Time was one thing they definitely had on their side. She would make this right. She had much to discuss with him. He had been born human, and with that infliction came a death sentence. All his acquaintances would die, and Seumas would be an eyewitness to their deaths. Serena desperately desired to save him from that torment and a lifetime of possible regret.

Fate had dealt this hand, and now, they'd have to make the best of it. He would acquire all knowledge from her. Which was more than she could say for others who had been turned. Left alone by their sire to fend for themselves. Not truly knowing what they were or what had become of them. That was their curse, and she would not let Seumas end up the same way. He would have full comprehension of what it means to be a vampire and the power of knowing you hold your captives life in your hands. He could easily take life as well as give it.

Serena kept a constant visual over Seumas and the way he reacted to all about him. She felt his hunger, but more than that, she felt his great love for his people.

Smiling, she could not have been put in this situation as a newly turned vamp and not drained every single one of them dry. He was the reason she had waited so long for a mate, for a companion. She felt proud, proud that she had chosen right.

He made her want to be a better person or in this case a better vamp, she was always on the edge of a double-bladed sword. A blade so sharp that it was hard to keep balance on, if she leaned too far to one side, she knew she would fall. She had been alone for so long, now, all she wanted was to be his in every way possible. She was desperate to be held by him for all eternity.

Time seemed to go by slowly as more and more of his clan visited him. Sitting in the wingback chair her eyes closed resting as she waited for all to leave. It had been hours since she had opened the door to Seumas's chamber and the waves of his people kept flooding the room. They seem to have come from all corners of his territory, his people showed their love for him. Soon the numbers began to dwindle and she found herself releasing a deep breath from her resting position. As she was about to speak, her lids flew open as the smell of lust filled her lungs, and it was a lust that didn't belong to them. The relief she felt moments ago was short lived, as the realisation came to her, there was a female still in his chamber. Serena took another deep breath to make sure she had smelt what she had. It most definitely was female though. The room was empty of all other smells, except for the primitive hunger. A snarl ripped from her chest as she recalled that scent.

Serena silently warned Seumas so he did not move from the bed. She rose from her seat and moved to where the smell came from. She felt the heartbeat and a desire so strong that it stirred her own craving. She knew who was hiding in the armoire, and she wanted nothing more than to yank her out by her hair.

Jealousy flared to life within her. As she neared the smell, the maid came to life within her mind. On a hiss, Serena reached for the armoire door. They both needed to be surprised to find her and at this moment, all she wanted was her blood. Serena never wanted anything more than to bleed her dry and use the maid's bones as wind chimes outside her chamber window. Although she could settle for smashing the poor maids face in. Taking a deep breath to steady her nerves.

Turning, she mouthed to him her plan. Only then did she speak. "Let me get ye fresh bedding, Seumas. Then, I shall assist ye over to the chair," she said as she turned back to the armoire.

She smiled as a squeal of alarm hit the air, and an embarrassed maid ran out, covering her face. Shame and blush so fierce caused her to hide her face in dismay as she fled the chamber.

The jealousy she felt did not go away. She had to know what this maid was to him, and she needed to know right now.

"Ye may move, my love," she hissed between clenched teeth. She had no right to feel this way. That knowledge did very little to help her. The desire to rip her apart still raged deep within her. She turned her attention to him now. "What is this woman to ye?" she asked, not trying to hide her anger.

There was no answer. Moving even closer to him, she asked again. Once again, there was no answer. Taking another step closer, she asked once more. This time, he reached out and pulled her down on the bed.

"The maid is of no one of importance."

The suspiciousness in her voice brought comfort to him. It meant more than she knew, showed how possessive she had become of him in such a short time. He felt the same way for her, only he would rip apart whoever or whatever wanted her. Nay other man would touch her or look at her in a manner that displeased him.

The answer he gave her did not please her, but he was not sure if he should tell her how intimately he knew the maid. Over the years since his wife's death, he'd had relations with the girl every now and again. Never letting her believe it was anything more than simple tupping. He'd only ever meant to scratch his itch, and that was few and far between. Yet it was now apparent to him that it meant more to the girl than it should. He should have known better, while he was not the man to indulge in her body, he was the first with any true authority.

"Ye are not telling me the truth, warrior. There's something between ye and her, isn't there?" she hissed up at him.

It was hard to keep her anger aflame as his hands roamed over her exposed flesh. But not wanting to give in to the sensations he stirred within her, she fought what he offered. She knew she would give in; there was no doubt. Just not right now.

"What's between the both of ye?" she asked as she wiggled beside him, trying desperately to free herself. Not that she truly wanted to be free. She knew she could have him on his back in a fraction of a second if she truly wanted to free herself. She would always be more powerful. She was older than him and with age came power, but as his maker, his blood would always recognise her and bend to her will.

The movements drove him crazy, and that was just how she wanted him. She wanted him crazed with need for her, so blind with sexual heat that he would do or say anything to get what he desperately craved. Even if he had to disclose all to her about his past sexual transgressions involving the maid.

Serena smirked to herself as a realisation dawned on her. She could almost see herself in some sleazy reality show, where she is confronting her wayward lover or husband about sleeping with the hired help as she demanded answers.

A fierce growl rumbled between them pulling her attention back to her warrior. His yearning grew stronger, filling the room with a thick blanket of musk. A scent which was purely all male.

She hungered for him. He could taste it in the air around them. The fact that she resisted her yearnings only heightened his desire. The knowledge that he could break her resistance with but one flick of his tongue drove him crazy with desire. The mere thought of that intimate caress caused his eyes to close. He'd had enough of this game, he would give her what she sought.

"Aye, ye are right to think something had taken place between the lass and me." He drew in a breath before he continued. What he was going to divulge would put him in a very unsavoury light. "I did nay force her into my bed. The girl came willingly. I did not bed her as often as ye might think, a mere handful of times," he said as he nuzzled behind her ear. "She was the means to satisfy the itch, when it got too strong I could not ignore it any longer. When the feel of my hand no longer eased the desire running wild within me. It did nay mean anything to me. Was nothing but tupping. I fear she might have wished it to be more than it ever would be."

"I agree with ye, Seumas. She does wish it to be more. Ye can smell it radiate from her," she said as she nipped at his neck. "Thank ye for telling me. It was hard for ye to tell me, so thank ye. Please know I would never pass judgement on ye for yer past actions. For I would not want to be judged for the wrongs and crimes I have committed," she whispered as she held his gaze.

All talking stopped as she gave in to her need for him as she placed a tender kiss on his luscious lips. Their bodies rubbing and grinding against each other. Yearning for more. Desperate to be flesh to flesh in pure, animalistic mating, all boundaries dropped. The predatory beasts within them given free rein, allowed to take their mate as they wished, to be truly free sexually, as clothes were ripped off of their bodies with little care given to them. The urge to be flesh to flesh drove them hard. A sigh escaped their lips as their skin met one another.

Seumas took in the swell of her full breast and the pebbling of her nipples as they called to him, begging for him to nip them, to suck them. Lowering himself to her heaving breast, drawing in a pebbled peak deep into the warmth of his mouth, rolling her nipple against his palate as his other hand played with her other breast. Her back arching into him as he gave her pleasure. Releasing her nipple with a pop as he looked into her passion filled eyes. His hand caressing every swell and curve of her body as he made his way to her moist heated core. His finger grazed her folds and the slickness they offered as he pumped two fingers deep inside her as he flicked his stiffened tongue over her bundle of nerves. His name moaned as her hand grasped at his hair desperate to hold him where she so desperately desired him. With every pass of his tongue, with every nibble given drove her wild with need. The vibration from his deep throaty growl of approval had her seeing stars.

Serena's eyes rolled to the back of her head at the first flick of his tongue. Her hips rolled against his mouth as he feasted on her core, riding his face as she sought out her pleasure. Her vision blurred as she closed her eyes tight. Starburst flashed behind her lids as her orgasm took over her body. Seumas held her to his mouth as she rode out her climax. Once her body went lax in his hands he climbed up her body and kissed her.

Serena moaned into his kiss as she tasted herself on his lips and tongue. She sucked and nipped at his lower lip. She kissed his jaw and his neck, stopping at a pulse point nipping at his lifeline. Seumas groaned as he felt her pierce his flesh. The smell of blood filled the air as their bodies joined as one. Blood beaded to the surface of skin that had been punctured. Pinpricks caused by sharp fangs as they bit into warm toned flesh. Punctures already started to heal. Leaving the smallest amount of evidence in its place.

The intense look in his eyes held her captive. Serena was unable to look away from Seumas's gaze, let alone close her eyes as he thrust deeper into her bodies' hot core. She moaned as she felt his long thick manhood fill her, stretching her feminine muscles to her limits, rocking her hips as she adjusted to his harsh intrusion. The slight bit of pain added to her budding desire.

The pleasure he gave her was beyond any she had ever known. He felt her every emotion and grew more boldly with his desire for her. Her gasps and moans caressed his very soul. Her silent pleas sent to him and him alone; her body begged him not to stop his attentions. He could no more stop the pleasuring of her than he could stop breathing.

Serena cried out his name as her orgasm blazed through her body. She wrapped herself more tightly around him as she rode every wave of pleasure he stroked out of her. He moaned as she pulled him deeper within her. He pounded into her as he sought his release, and with a few more thrusts, he climaxed, calling out her name as she milked every last drop of his seed. It was only then did he realise blood filled his mouth, causing him to spill his seed once more.

Serena felt his amazement with his new body as she fed on his blood. Blood so pure that she wanted more. She did not think she would ever get enough of him. She would never get enough of his blood and his person, he is her drug of choice. It was a good thing that they now had all of eternity together.

She absorbed his weight willingly as his body went lax in her arms. They lay, sated, in each other's arms.

Rolling to his side, he gently pulled her with him, tucking her body closely to his. Not yet willing to give up the heat they shared together.

Chapter Twenty Seven

The day turned to night and nights to days and days to weeks. They took this time to learn from each other. Of their bodies and their minds, but it was more than that. It was their very souls they seemed to explore. She gave of herself freely, as did he. Both were desperate to fully know what was within, no corner left untouched, no dark shadow unexplored. Every square inch was explored and talked about freely until there was nothing left to say between them. Nothing left to hide, free to be themselves. Until nothing but love, respect, and understanding blossomed around them.

So went their days and nights with the smallest of interruptions from his people. The intrusion into their world was brief but felt all the same.

Their days were filled with visits from his clansmen and kinsmen alike. All happy to see their lord up and moving about, all boasting of his rapid healing spread and how the MacIver's bloodline is strong and cannot be defeated easily blazes like wildfire throughout the villagers. Little did they know just how quickly his healing truly was.

William and Kari also found each night brought them to Seumas's chamber. It was a visit all looked forward to.

As the men talked in great length about what had transpired that day, the women found they, too, fell into a routine as well. Serena's mind was distracted for a time by the company of her good friend, Kari offered. As she got to know the lady that lay behind the eyes, she found the name Kari fitted her much more than Kar. Kari gave her a sense of elegance, a regal quality that befitted her and her gentle soul.

She shone as a student under her care. She taught her all that she knew of the scholarly world. To her delight, she was a very fast learner, eager to learn as much as she could. A small smile curved upon her lips as she set the book aside she was currently reading. Kari was a woman who would make a name for herself in Serena's modern world. A world she would be frightened of at first, but in the end, she would conquer it, leaving her mark on all she did. Yet still came home to the warm embrace of her lover and the tenderness he offered.

Seumas and William more often than not found their gazes settling on their ladies. Eventually, they would give up the fight, adjusting their chairs accordingly sitting as they watch the interaction between their women. And so went their nights until the urge to take what they so richly craved took hold of them. This night was no different. Well, except in one way.

Before Seumas knew what was happening, he had Serena in his arms, kissing her deeply, his hand fisted in her hair. His yearning for her more than he could withhold, and he did not care who saw their most intimate of moments. He needed her for all eternity, not only as his mate but also as his beloved wife. Easing his kiss, he gently repositioned her in his lap as he sat. Not caring if the intimacy he shared with his woman upset William's woman or not. That thought did not last long, as William intended to do the same.

It was at that moment that he found his voice. "Lass," he whispered for only her to hear. Seumas wanted desperately to find the softness that he held deep within himself. A tenderness which only she brought out within him. Once he held that in his heart, only then would he speak. "There is something I wish to ask ye." A wealth of emotion laced in his words.

Their gazes met and held. Serena took in a breath at what she saw in his eyes. A fire burned deep within the depths of his eyes, and she was unable to look away, not that she ever would.

"Serena, my love. Marry me. Be my wife. Be mine forever. Fill my life and my keep with love, laughter, and children," he asked of her as he placed a soft kiss upon her lips.

Easing away from her, Seumas waited for her response, and it felt like a lifetime.

His words touched her more than she had expected them to. She had waited so long to hear those two words; they took her breath away. What was she waiting for? Why had she not shouted her answer to him?

Coming out of her shock, she quickly found her voice. "Yes. Yes, I will marry you. I give myself to you forever," she about shouted as she embraced him in a fierce hug, tears brimming her eyelids.

Everything she had dreamed of for so long was coming true. Not only had she found the life she wanted, but her life mate as well. Just one thing was missing now—the Heffernan's. That, too, would soon be remedied. They discussed the topic of her friends, and he felt they would have the answers they sought.

Seumas stood holding Serena tight to his body wanting to fully feel her body against his, a body that would soon be forever his. This was what he had waited for all these long years he spent alone, someone to call his once more. Biding his time until a true mate came along. Seumas was pulled from his thoughts by the congratulation they received from their friends. He no longer needed the crystal to see what he now held in his heart, yet he still needed it. There was much in his clan that still needed to be clarified with the crystals' help. He would not ponder on it now, for he had far happier thoughts to indulge himself in.

Tonight, once William and Kari retired for the eve, they'd slip out of the keep to celebrate their soon-to-be marriage. To make merry in a way that was pleasurable to the creature within. Let the savage beast within run free, to hunt and feed in all its glory. To truly be one with its mate.

A smell drifted across the winds catching their attention, their heads snapping in the direction of the mouth watering aroma. They gave chase going deep into the nearby woods as the hunt gripped them. The pounding of the stag's hooves as it hit the earth as it fled for its life stirred the primal beast within. They bounded over fallen trees and boulders as they went deeper in the forest leaping over streams. They came to a halt as they crouched down hiding themselves behind a large log as they watched the stag come to a stop as it searched its surroundings. Its breath comes out in white puffs of steam as it heaves in its stance, drawing in the much needed air after the distance it was forced to travel. The stag's heart beats rapidly in its chest as it tries to regain its calmness.

Their beast within them took over as they leapt over the log tackling the stag with a force causing it to stagger before regaining its balance. They fought for dominance, and survival. One fighting for its life and the others fighting to take it. They felt it weakening, tiring out as it gave up the fight as Serena and Seumas bit into its flesh draining it of its lifeforce. Even after this kill the hide and the flesh will be put to good use. The carcass would be skinned and stretched. The skin left to dry for its leather and the meat portioned amongst his clan.. He would instruct his clan on where to go to claim the animal once they were back at the keep.

As the night went on, Seumas sat with his woman in his lap, refusing to give up the comfort it brought. With a broad smile on his face, he listened to the women making plans for his soon-to-be wedding. If he had it his way, they would be wed tonight—or at the utmost, five days.

Knowing that was not possible, he would have to wait until preparations were made and met. The wedding banns had to be announced three times before the marriage could take place. Only he knew there was no one to object to the marriage taking place. There is no legal reason for any to oppose their union.

Serena hid her smile from all to see. She felt exactly what her soon-to-be husband was thinking, and she had to smile. It was absolutely like her warrior to be impatient when it came to the things he wanted, and he most definitely coveted her. Too bad he was going to have to wait to claim her as wife. She always dreamed of her wedding day, and now that one was coming, she desired to do it right, follow all the laws set in place in his time.

She didn't want a modern-day celebration for her wedding. No, she desired a true thirteenth-century ceremony, right down to the chapel. She could see him in his full Scottish regalia garb and her in a long, flowing gown. Fresh heather, mixed with wildflowers, simply tied with ribbons for a bouquet. Oh, yes, she could see it all, and she wanted it. She never truly knew how badly she wanted it until now. She tasted it, and she could say without a doubt that she would kill to have it. And she just might have to if they found them out.

She believed they would accept them for what she was and for what he had become. He had not truly changed. Seumas was still the person he had been but with a small, insignificant difference. Should it matter that, instead of food, he required blood for nourishment? Food gave some, but not enough. He was still able to keep up pretence, keeping an air of normalcy about him. But blood would be the one thing he could not live without. If he tried, he would become ravenousness for blood and kill all in sight. It would not matter if they were young or old as long as he got blood. In the aftermath, the realisation of what he had done would hit, and grief would follow.

For now, she was going to focus on happy thoughts. She would focus on her soon-to-be wedding, a wedding she thought would never come, even now Serena could not believe it. After nine hundred–odd years she was finally going to be married.

MARRIED! MARRIED!

She was still not able to wrap her head around the idea. Her mind telling her not to believe in fairy tales and her heart shouting for her to grab hold of him and never let him go. She was going with her heart on this one. Her mind would eventually catch up to her heart.

The days that followed were some of the happiest days and nights of her life. They spent time together and apart, making arrangements for their wedding. The household staff buzzing with happiness, they took over the arrangements for their lord and soon-to-be mistress. The kitchen staff cooked and baked nonstop, preparing for the breakfast feast.

She felt a pinch of guilt for all the hard work the household staff had to do. There was no budging Seumas on the time frame. He simply would not wait a month to be married to her, a fortnight was all he was willing to agree to. Two weeks. Two measly weeks he had granted them to plan a wedding. Seumas reassuring her their staff was more than up to the task. She should have never doubted him. The staff went to work, planning, decorating, and cooking, putting modern-day wedding planers to shame. Somehow, in the midst of it all, they found the time to make her a wedding dress.

It was more than a wedding dress. It was everything she had ever dreamed of for her wedding gown. A gown which befitted a queen, their acceptance and love for her touched her heart. Somewhere between her saving the lord and becoming his soon-to-be bride, she had won the hearts of his people.

That thought kept her company at night. William and Kari kept them apart at night. Both made sure they stayed in their own chambers. They even went as far as to put guards at their doors. Both guards were given strict orders by William not to obey either one of them. Nights were the hardest for them both. The only plus side was their connection to each other.

The first few nights apart, Seumas took it with good humour. As time went on, she felt his frustration and his rising hunger. Then, it subsided. It was on the next morning that she saw William with fresh marks on his arm. She could not let him continue to do this. She would have to talk to William about this. That was the last thing she thought when she heard a scream and the sense of panic radiating off her warrior. No one seemed to be reacting to the scream, but she heard it. She knew she heard it.

Seumas reached out to her. *"Lass, I have need of ye now. The maid has seen. I put her in a trance. She will be awakening soon. Come to me at once."*

"Coming, my warrior. Hold on, my love. Don't panic."

Don't panic. Don't panic. Now was the perfect time to panic. She knew it was only a matter of time before someone found out their secret.

She had to get into his room, but she could not use the door. Even with her speed, the guards would be sure to notice the doors open and close, causing them to look into her chamber and his. The window was her only true option, one she hated to use. For one never knew who was down below, and that in itself could cause a huge dilemma. It was a chance she had to risk. Before she knew it, she was out the window and on the ground. Now, she had to hope none were around to see her. Drawing on her power of speed, she made her way around to his window. Serena scanned the area looking for any prying eyes before she committed herself to air once more, landing on her warrior's windowsill with a sigh of relief.

The scene she found herself jumping into was something straight out of a Bram Stoker's novel. The wild look in Seuma's eyes, was the kind of look of a cornered deer, one that had nowhere else to run, nowhere left to hide as it fought for control over its fear. There Seumas stood with the body of the maid limp in his arms as he stood in front of the fire. Her blood coating his flesh crimson as it dripped from his fangs onto his lovely, broad chest, staining his pristine white shirt as it continued to run down his chest.

William slumped in a chair with a look of hope in his eyes. Hope that all will be all right. She could only pray that it would be.

"What happened here? How did she come to be in your chamber at this hour of the night?"

Serena watched as both men glanced at the armoire. *Not again* – she thought with a sigh. That stupid little bitch had hidden in the armoire once again. She did not want to ask her next question but knew deep down that she had to. If she was going to fix the situation she needed all the information she could get her hands on.

"Whose blood is this?" she questioned as she gestured to his person. Knowing full well what the response would be.

He did not disappoint.

" 'Tis the lass's blood."

Serena turned her gaze to William as she let her eyes run over his slumped form, as she looked for the fresh marks she knew would be on William's flesh.

It was as she thought, and she knew this could only go two ways and she prayed for the best. She would give her warrior the options and let him decide. She thought as she pinched the bridge of her nose.

"We have two choices in this situation. First, drain her dry and bury her body somewhere not to be found, or second, compel her to make her forget. I must warn ye though that there's a chance that she shall remember all that happened here if the compelling is not strong enough."

A sigh escaped her lips. There was a very large chance that this could happen. A person's mind was a maze of wiring and hard to control, let alone trying to block out a memory was damn near impossible. Yet Serena was willing to try to bend time itself if it meant saving her warrior. Compared to bending time, a little erasing of the mind seemed like a piece of cake.

"Let us start, Seumas. William, ye are to keep watch."

"Aye, milady."

First thing first, she had to wake the maid up. At least she would get some kind of satisfaction out of this she thought with a grin on her face, as she slapped her hard across the unconscious maids face. Serena needed to look into her eyes for this to work, for them to even have a chance. The maid roused from her forced slumber with a look of confusion etched on her face for a split second before she freaked-out.

Serena took swift control over the maid before she drew unwanted attention from the guards outside the door. Serena took hold of the maids head staring deep into the hazel eyes before her.

"What is her name," she asked as she held eye contact with the woman in front of her.

"Margot. Her name is Margot MacTavish," said Seumas with regret in his voice. She did not have time to ease his mind and heart at the moment.

"Margot, ye are going to listen to me and only me. Hear my voice and nothing else. I want ye to keep looking into my eyes. That's a good girl. I want ye to think about the loch as ye sit and watch the calmness the water offers. The full moon is shining above ye and its light is reflecting off the water of the loch. There is a cool breeze causing ye to shiver and wrap yer shawl around ye a little tighter. Ye feel a hand on yer shoulder and ye look up into the eyes of yer father. He sits ye and ye talk about a boy he wants ye to marry. He desires ye to be happy and taken care of. Ye agree to the marriage," Serena says as she takes a deep breath. She created the story and now she has to remove what she saw from her memory. "Margot, ye will have no recollection of what happened here tonight in yer Lords chamber. Ye never hid in the armoire and ye did not see him feed off of William or ye. Ye have never seen him naked and have never kissed or touched him. He is only yer lord and that is all he is to ye. Nod yer head if ye understand what I am telling ye," Serena said as she glanced up at both men. She felt the nod of her head in understanding. Serena did not know how long she had been compelling Mrgot for, but she felt the fatigue kicking in. "Okay Margot, I'm going to count backwards from five and when I get to one ye will awaken and not remember what happened. Five, four, three, two, one. Awaken," she said, moving away from the maid.

"Milord, do ye need anything before I retire for the night," she asked with a little bob of her head.

Coming out of his shock enough of him to answer her. "Nay, Margot. Ye may seek yer rest for the night," he said as he moved towards the door.

There was a collective intake of breath from them all as he closed the door behind her.

"We shall discuss this on a later date. This cannot happen again. Do ye understand me," she said looking them both in their eyes. With a nod from them both she made her way over to the window. She had to get back to her room before Kari showed up for her nightly visit.

Chapter Twenty Eight

Time ticked by swiftly, and the day of their wedding was now upon them. It was a day they both were looking forward to, she knew Seumas was biting at the bit to have her in his arms once more. Time alone became harder to come by, as they had to keep watch on the maid. There seemed to be no repercussions from the night of the incident. For they all knew all they could do was pray for the glamour to hold.

Serena still recalling how long and hard that night was for her. The long, gruelling hours she worked into the night desperately tried to erase the memories from the maid's mind. Not only to expunge the memories of her warrior drinking her precious lifeblood, but of Seumas and William as well.

Compelling was not as easy as some would think in her modern world, and it sure as hell was not easy in mediaeval Scotland. The people of this time held very strong, rooted beliefs. Beliefs held in spiritual and demonic forces. And their kind would be considered demonic more so than angelic. So, there was no simple effort on her part. It was not as elementary as compelling the soul to believe in what ye told them. No, she could not have it so effortlessly. She had to go through every part of her mind and scrub it clean, so to speak. Once sure she had accomplished that feat, only then did she replace memories, and that took as much time as wiping one's memory clean.

The girl was not the only thing on her mind at the moment. She had yet to find the time to talk to William and Seumas about the feedings. Feedings that had become more and more frequent. Now, it was much more than feedings. There was longing in William's eyes, a yearning to be more than mortal. He held a look in his eyes that graced all of those mortals that lined the walls of immortal clubs. Desire to be more. The call of immortality beckoned them like a drug. A drug they could not withstand. Nor did they want to. Everything about immortals drew them to the lifestyle. Now, William was one of the many with the yearning for forever. To have forever in the arms of his lover. She could not blame him for that desire. She, too, had wanted that. The knowledge of being alone was what had driven her to change Seumas. She knew in her heart that she would have turned him even if he had been ready to die. For her, there was no life, no forever without him, and she had been more than willing to risk her happiness. Even if it meant an eternity of him hating her, at least he would be alive. And she would take her happiness in knowing he still lived.

This was not going to be easy. If she turned one, she would have to turn the other. This was not what she wanted. She did not want to start her own coven, conscious of the fact that it would not stop there. She was going to have to broach the subject soon, but not today. Today was their day. *Their day*. The sound of it made her heart soar. This was the beginning of their forever. They would be man and wife by the end of this day. Life had taken a turn for the better, and she wanted to bathe in all its glory.

She stood in the middle of her chamber, gazing into a mirror, as servants buzzed around her. She had been washed and oiled in a very intimate way. If she were a maiden, she could imagine the profuse blush that would now grace her cheeks. All knew well that she warmed her lord's bed, yet none said anything about it. Instead, she found herself on the receiving end of sexual advice. Even now, with all the sexual partners she'd had, she found herself completely intrigued by the advice they gave her. She had not expected such openness on this subject. These women must have been bold lovers in their younger days and probably still were.

Serena became lost in her thoughts as the women chatted around her, before she knew it, she stood in front of the full-length mirror, fully dressed in her wedding gown. Disbelief filled her. This woman that stood before the looking glass in complete amazement was not real. At least, not to her. This had not been her in a very long time. Serena wanted desperately to be this again more than anything. To be true to herself once more. This was who she was and meant to be. All she needed to do was say those two little words that would change her life forever—

I do. Loving the way it sounded on her lips. She was ready. Ready to start her life with her bonded mate.

"Ye ready, milady?"

"Aye, I am more than ready. Shall we make our way to the chapel?"

"Nay, not yet. We still have some time. I wish to convey me regard to ye and me lord. Wish ye both a very merry and long life."

It was the *long life* part that got her. It felt as if she was trying to tell her that she knew. Not only that she knew, but also that she was more than okay with it. She was not sure if she should clarify this with her. Mayhap she would test the waters.

"Thank ye for yer best wishes. It means more to me than ye know. I feel as though ye are trying to tell me something and just do not know how to broach the subject." She guessed right by her reaction. "Ye may ask me about whatever ye wish. I shall answer ye if I can. I might not know the answer to what ye ask. But I shall try to respond if possible, so please ask me what ye will."

She watched as the woman worked up the muster to ask what was on her mind. To her delight, she did not have to wait long.

"How was it possible for ye to save the lord? He should have died. Please, do nay misunderstand me. We are all very grateful for ye saving him. I but wonder how such a thing is possible, that is all."

"The only answer I can give ye is, I am a healer of sorts. I have the ability to bring people back from near death." Praying that the answer she gave would suffice the lady standing before her. She was not exactly ready to announce to all and sundry that she was Nosferatu, the undead, thriving on the blood of others—at least, not on her wedding day.

A hatred so deep took hold of her, it was a loathing that started from the moment she had told her first falsehood. Serena grew weary of the falsehoods she told. Mayhap a coven of her making would not be so bad. Would make her world a whole lot easier, no need for lies any longer. A coven had merit, a definite advantage worthy of bloodshed. It gave her something to think about.

"Milady, thank ye for yer honesty," she said as she embraced her in a hug. " 'Tis time to go to the chapel. Ye look so very beautiful. Milord is going to be very pleased. He's done well in choosing ye for his bride."

"Thank ye. Now, let us go. I do not wish to keep Seumas waiting." Taking one last long look in the mirror, simply admiring her beauty. Before she turned on her heels, heading for the door and her future at hand.

Over the last hour, he made adjustments to his Highland garb, straightening and adjusting the pleats of his kilt once more. He did nay think it possible for him to be nervous, yet he was—or was he? Seumas was not sure if it was the nervousness he was feeling or if he purely wanted to get his new life started with his bride, a life that had been put on hold for far too long.

Seumas was more than ready for his new life to begin. Welcoming the right to take his wife in his arms when and where he wanted to without the unapproving glances. There would be no more hiding behind closed doors. Very soon, he would have the right to kiss her in full view of all, if he so wished. At the moment he desired to do more than just kiss her. It had been too long for him in the taking of his woman.

He had not held her in his arms since that fateful night of the chambermaid. They saw one another in passing, and when lucky, on occasion, she would be alone long enough for him to steal a kiss or two, but that was it. The passion they shared in his bed had been halted, and all he yearned or thought of was her in his bed. He wanted to take her in every way a man could take a woman, and his list was long, so very long. The rogue in him wanted nothing more than to be free, to ravish his woman in any way he pleased. To command her to do things that only she could perform.

The memory of her dancing for him and the things she did were all that kept him company at night. Well, that was not all that kept him company. Along with the images of her came his throbbing, raging manhood. His manhood was not the only thing that throbbed. He could feel his fangs elongate and pulse in his need. Even now, he controlled his needs from the mere smell of her.

This aside, he had to clear his mind, for he could not go to the chapel with the proof of his desire for all to see. He would have to adjust his kilt once more and do some thinking on anything other than his woman. The knock on his door drew his attention.

"Milord, 'tis time to make our way to the chapel. Ye do not wish to keep yer bride waiting, do ye?" said William as he entered. "I see that ye are eager for yer bride, milord," said William in between his laughter. "I nay think it acceptable for ye to enter the chapel as ye are. Ye must take care of this now, milord. Ye do nay have the time to wait for it to go down. I shall give ye time. I shall be but outside yer door. I suggest ye be quick about it," he said over his shoulder as he headed for the chamber door.

Seumas knew William was right. He'd had this problem for the last few days now, and the matter did nay seem to want to resolve itself. He did the only thing he could do; he closed his eyes and pictured his woman's shapely curves as he wrapped his fingers around his hard shaft. His hand took on a life of its own as the images of Serena became more and more provocative. The head of his shaft throbbed, seeping fluid as he neared his release. He quickened his pace and threw his head back as the image of her fangs piercing his flesh excited him. His groans vibrated off the walls as his orgasm tore through him. Bracing himself against the wall, he worked every last drop of his seed out of his shaft, ensuring his full release. Resting his head against the wall, he drew deep breaths to steady himself once more. The rap on the door drew his attention. Time to go. Dropping his kilt back into place, he pulled away from the wall. He would not keep his bride waiting. A quick wash, and he was out the door.

"Milord, we must leave now. Milady will arrive at the chapel soon."

Seumas did not answer; instead, he opened his chamber door and closed it behind him. "Once the wedding ceremony ends, William, I want ye to send a maid up to our chamber to make sure all is in order."

"I shall take care of it, milord. Ye can be sure of it. Now, let us get to yer wedding."

They made it to the chapel with time to spare, a welcome sight. At one glance around, he knew all had worked hard to decorate the inside. It was not only the decorations that touched his heart, but also the full chapel, every pew and outer walkway filled. It showed how much they cared for them both. That knowledge touched him more than he could say.

As he made his way up the aisle to the altar, he noticed the priest entering from the side room. He wanted to thank the man of the cloth for holding the wedding so quickly, even though it went against church laws. Knowing it was customary for banns to be called out, and signed agreements from her kinsmen set in place. It was her kinsmen's right to give her hand in marriage, to agree to this union between them. There was no need for banns to be called out, for there would be no objections. There were nay kinsmen for the Kirk to send requests to. And the only agreements that need be honored were between them.

"Milord, over yonder, on the small table, is the marriage documents. Ye and milady may sign them before or after the wedding."

"Milady and I shall be signing after our vows have been given. I shall, however, read over the agreements now," he said as he walked over to the small table, the Latin simply phrased and straightforward.

Chapter Twenty Nine

The buzz in the chapel carried into the rafters. All were merry as they spoke among one another, all awaiting the bride to arrive. It had been far too long since he had seen his people happy. They longed for him to remarry. Longed for the clan to be complete, to be whole once more. As did he, and this time, there would be no death. They would have a love that lived forever. With that thought, he closed his eyes and reached for Serena. The link they shared through their minds was his safe haven while they were apart. He needed to touch her mind once more to feel her near.

Serena had counted and counted over and over again in her head all the times Seumas crossed her mind, every thought she had to use her power of speed and enter the chapel doors like a crazed banshee from hell. To her, it felt as if she was moving at a snail's pace, and she felt her impatience quickly boiling over the edge. The deep urge to be with her mate, to be near him, drove her closer and closer to the edge. To run at full speed, throw the chapel doors wide, and demand the priest to be quick with the vows. She knew this was not possible. Then, she felt his touch caress her mind. Serena inhaled deeply to calm herself and her raging hormones ran wild within her.

Dazed from the caress, Serena felt like she had been drugged and she was coming down from her high. And she wanted her next fix, needed to be with her mate. She had known this would happen, but she did not think it would happen this quickly. Her body demanded his blood, and only his blood would do. Her needs were going to have to wait. Her soul was far more pressing, and right now, it required her warrior's heart.

"Here we be, milady. Now, let's take one last look at ye. Oh… milord is going to beam when he sees ye," she said as she clasped her hands to her full, round breasts.

Unable to say anything, she stood in front of the chapel doors, waiting for the right moment to move. Then, she smelled him, could almost taste him on the winds. His voice was a low purr in her mind as he reached out to her, and she wanted all he offered.

"Milady, 'tis time." With that said, she opened the doors wide and led Serena in.

Seumas smelled her before he could see and feel her. The early dawn light shone in like a beacon as the doors to the chapel opened wide. Light cascaded around her, hiding her from his sight for the briefest of moments. All he saw was the outline of her. His Serena looked to be an angel, and very soon, he would have the right to claim her. She was his prize after all these years of torment.

A collective gasp came from all in the chapel as the doors closed behind her. She was beyond breathtaking. At that moment, he held nothing but pride in his heart. Aye, fate had been very kind to him when she brought Serena to him. This was the life he was meant to live. Fate had known it all along and taken what was not meant to be. Setting things right once more.

"Magnificent, milord," whispered William. He could see the love Seumas held for his woman. A love that was pure and true.

"Aye, she is," he said, not taking his eyes off of her. Not chancing a second of lost time between them, he did not want to lose a second or minute of the vision before him.

Reaching his side, he took her hand in his and brought it to his lips. Placing the gentlest of kisses on her knuckles. "Ye are very lovely, my dear," he purred, holding her gaze.

But it was what she saw in his eyes that got her blood and lust running hot. There was a great deal of promises in his eyes, and she desired it. Yearned for it all, right down to every unspoken promise. A promise held only for her.

They stood before the priest, listened to every word said in Latin. The ceremony seemed to take a lifetime, as all things in Latin did. Finally, their time to say their vows to each other, vows that would forever bind them together in the eyes of God.

"Do ye, Seumas MacIver, take Serena Wulff to be yer wife, to have and to hold, until death do ye part?"

"I do," said Seumas without hesitation. There would never be hesitation in his heart when it came to her. He would give his life for hers if it meant she lived.

"And do ye, Serena Wulff, take Seumas MacIver to be ye lawfully wedded husband from this day forward, for richer, for poorer, in sickness and in health, until death shall ye part?"

"I do, with all my heart," she said as tears slipped from her eyes down her cheeks.

"I now pronounce ye man and wife. Ye may kiss your bride."

Engulfing his wife in his arms, he kissed her gently on her full lips. He tasted the desire for more within her, and he would give her what she wanted and more.

She is going to have to wait a little bit longer, he thought as he let his fangs graze over her lips.

The shiver that ran down her back only heightened his yearning. How he was going to hate ruining her lovely gown. Ruined it shall be.

"Forever," he whispered for only her to hear.

"Forever," she murmured as she stepped away.

"I introduce to all present here before God the new Lord and Lady MacIver," said the priest for all to hear within the chapel. "May they have a long and happy life together."

All in the chapel came to their feet as the newly married couple walked down the aisle, showering them with seeds and grains, wishing them a large family.

"Nay worry, milord, milady, for I have a carriage awaiting ye just over here. I thought ye might need some privacy. The wedding party shall meet ye at the keep."

"Thank ye, William," Serena said as she placed a kiss on his cheek. "Ye will make Kari a fine husband one day soon."

"Thank ye, milady."

"There is no reason to thank me, William. I am telling ye what I know to be true. We will see ye at the keep."

"Aye, William, we will see ye at the keep. Do not rush," he said with a wink and a very wicked laugh. "Come, wife. Let us leave before the sun is too high."

Serena did not need any further encouragement from her husband. More than ready to leave and have her alone time with her husband.

"Come, love," he said as he took her hand, helping her into the carriage. Watching her through hooded lids.

His lust for his wife was too new and raw to control, and the ride to the keep was going to prove interesting, he thought as he closed the carriage door behind them. She sat as demurely as a modest, shy, untouched virgin. Her hands gently folded in her lap and her head bowed, hiding her face from his sight. The picture she portrayed was exactly that—a picture. For he knew under the surface of the demure image lay a predator. And that was whom he wanted to play with. That was the woman he desired to taste. The image it conjured up had his fangs throbbing.

"I can smell the lust radiating off of ye, husband," she said, still not lifting her head. "Ye could not imagine what the smell of yer lust does to me," she purred as she moved her hair, exposing the column of her neck. "So, my warrior, was this what ye wanted, or was there something richer ye desire?" she said, thrusting her chest toward him in open invitation.

"Be careful in what ye offer me, wife. Been far too long since I felt or tasted yer flesh," he said with a low growl. "Ye do have something that I want at this moment," he said as he moved forward in his seat, running his fingers over her décolleté and down the slope of her breast. His fingers slipped even lower until he reached the spot he wanted. "There is where I wish to taste," he said as he applied the gentlest of pressure right above her heart.

Serena felt the wetness between her thighs increase as she listened to her husband's sweet threats. She could almost feel his fangs sink deep into her sweet spot.

"Take me," was all she was able to get out before she found herself pinned under her husband's weight. A weight she was more than willing to bear for all eternity.

"Ye have teased me enough, wife," he murmured as he traced her ear to nuzzle the hollow behind it. He felt her pulse quicken as her blood heated with passion. His hands sought the hem of her gown, desperate to feel her soft, supple skin. To feel the moisture he knew was there. To have her honeyed cream run down his hand as she climaxed.

A low growl rumbled in his chest as he touched her flesh and the full force of her honey engulfed him. The sweet smell of her wantonness hit him like a ton of bricks. He would have been sent to his knees if he were standing. He thanked the heavens for small favours, for he already was on his knees, worshipping his goddess.

Capturing her lips once more in a fierce, demanding kiss, he slipped two fingers deep inside of her.

"I sense yer pleasure, wife. Was this what ye needed, or would ye like it faster and harder?" he asked as he licked her life-giving artery. He knew she could not answer, as her panting had quickened. "That's it, wife. Do nay hold back. Give me what I seek," he whispered as he hastened his speed.

Serena did not want this sweet torment to stop, she never had a lover that made her feel this way. But then none had ever been Seumas. All thoughts stopped as her climax drew near, she reached for her husband's manhood, needing desperately to be one with him. And she knew they had very little time left before reaching the keep.

"Seumas, my love, I need to be one with ye now," she said as she turned the tables on him and straddled him. Serena joined their bodies in one swift motion, taking in his thick length deep within her. She rocked her hips painfully slow at first, as she simply enjoyed the feel of being one with her husband. It did not take long for them to get lost in the demands of their bodies. Their moans blending together as they worked for their release, demanding of each other's body to give what they so richly craved.

Serena cried out with her release as her body contracted around his hard shaft. Her fangs elongated as she rode out her climax. She yearned for his blood—and now. Sinking her fangs into his exposed flesh, she drew urgent, deep pulls from him. A purr deep in her throat vibrated as his blood coated the palate of her mouth. It was at that moment that his blood tasted ever so sweet, the moment of his body's surrender.

Seumas came hard over and over again the moment he felt her fangs sink deep. He thrust deep inside of her, ensuring his seed warmed her womb. His fangs sank deep within her flesh as he rode out every spasm bursting free from his cock. He drew of her lifeblood as he filled her womb. This woman in his arms suited him far more than any he had ever held.

Mine, was the last coherent thought he had

Chapter Thirty

William sat, watching his friends make merry, and dreamed of one day doing the same with his woman. A woman who meant the world to him. One day, they would have the same, and he prayed for it to be soon.

He noticed the small red marks that now graced their necks and knew at once what they had shared in the carriage. He knew those marks well, and he craved to have them. William yearned to be one of them, he longed for forever, longed for eternity with Kari. An eternity with the one he loved in his arms and his bed.

It was at that moment that Serena and Seumas felt the energy change around William. Felt the hunger of his desperation. An eagerness for more time, and it was that deep desperation that brought them to their decision. Looking in his direction, Seumas gestured for him to come over to them. He knew that Serena held the key to what William desired.

William searched their faces for any hint of what might be on their minds. There was a solemn expression and seriousness focused on him and only him. Then, a smile graced their faces, and their eyes lit up as if they were hopeful of what he would say or do. Yet he could not conceive what they wanted to discuss with him on this happy day.

For them to gesture him over at such a time, it must be of importance, he thought as he made his way over to the high table.

"Milord, milady. Ye wish to speak to me?" said William in a curious tone he could not hide.

"Aye, William, we do. Please sit down here," he said as he lifted his wife into his lap, offering William her now-empty chair. "We have something of importance to discuss with ye and Kari. Mayhap ye should go fetch yer woman first. For it involves the both of yer future," he said as he looked into his wife's exquisite face. "Go fetch yer woman, but be quick about it."

"Aye, at once, milord, milady." His hopes ran high as he thought about what had been said.

Could his Kari become his wife sooner than he thought? Her husband had been dead only a short while, and it was customary for the widow to remain unmarried for a year. Had Seumas come up with a plan to overrule the law and allow them to wed? He prayed this was the case.

"There ye are, sweetling," he said as he smelled her hair. "I have been looking everywhere for ye."

"I am sorry. I found I needed fresh air," she whispered as she leaned into his embrace. "What is it ye need of me?" she murmured.

"Come, sweetling. Our lord and ladyship wish to speak with us." He could not hide his enthusiasm. "Come. We must get back."

Kari allowed herself to be gently tugged toward the keep doors. William's eagerness quickly infecting her own, soon, she found herself running beside him, trying to keep up. She had never seen him like this. It got her wondering what the lord and ladyship wanted. She knew it had to be something wonderful. She and Serena had spent a lot of time together before her wedding day. Over that time, they talked about a great number of things. All of which had given her considerable hope. She tried to recollect all of their conversations and the topic of them. Then, it came to her; they all centred on William. She picked up her pace, not wanting to keep them waiting any longer.

Together William and Kari found themselves seated at the high table, Kari finding it hard to stay still, almost bouncing in her chair with built up excitement.

"Ah... good, William, ye found her. Now, we can begin to talk about yer future together," announced Seumas.

He knew that statement got both of their attention at once. It was a statement meant to capture their interest and pique their curiosity. And it did just that.

"Now that I have gotten yer undivided attention, we would like to talk to ye both about yer relationship," said Seumas. "I think it best if my wife does the speaking. I know well that Kari and she have spent much time together. So, it only seems fitting that she talk now," he murmured as he placed a kiss on his wife's hand.

Who was she to broach the topic of vampirism to a woman who held deep religious beliefs? Kari knew what she was, but accepting her for whom and what she was, was different from becoming one. Would she take it, or would she walk away from what she offered and the love William gave her? Only one way to find out, and that was to ask.

Taking a deep breath, she looked at William, and the love he held in his eyes for his woman gave her the courage to proceed. This was it. There was no turning back now.

"William, Kari, I know the love ye have for each other runs deep and true. Anybody around ye two sees the love between ye. The both of ye were meant to be together. The question is, for how long? Will ye have five or ten years together, maybe longer if ye are lucky? We all know the harshness of the world we live in and how quickly the loved ones in yer life could be taken away. The world is cruel, and ye do not know when or where death shall claim ye," she said as she searched their eyes for any hint of emotion.

There it is, she thought as tears rolled down Kari's cheeks.

She did not want to make her cry, but she knew it was necessary. The only way for Kari to set aside her religious beliefs and turn was to show no mercy. She did it with no mercy, with no remorse.

"I know what I am saying hurts, but it's the truth, and ye must face it and face it now," she said as she looked over her shoulder to her husband.

He gave her a little nod of his head to urge her on.

"Ye need to go on, my love. Ye are breaking through to her. It's for her own good. Ye know this to be the only way. She'll forgive ye for what ye are saying. 'Tis the only way for them to be together forever. 'Tis the only way they'll have true happiness," he murmured in her mind.

Serena squeezed his hand to let him know she understood what he was telling her. Seumas tightened his hold on her hand, for he knew this was not easy for her to talk about in the open. It went against everything she had ever been taught. It went against her survival instinct to keep from revealing her innermost secrets. Yet she continued on with her talk. Always brave. No fear in her heart. She would always make him proud.

She looked into William's eyes and saw the hope brighten. He knew where she was going with this and was more than ready to take the leap. He was ready to take that jump to eternity. It was not him she was trying to convince, but his very lovely woman.

"What I am offering is an eternity in each other's arms. An eternity to make up for lost happiness. Do ye understand what I am telling you, Kari? What I offer both of ye? All ye must do is turn," she whispered as she reached for her hands, taking note of the slight tremble in them.

Was the tremble from fear or anticipation of what had been said?

"Let me turn ye. Convert ye to be a vampire. Become as Seumas has become. Live, Kari. Live the life ye were meant to live. The life that was taken away from ye when ye married the wrong man. Live, Kari. Live and love the man that loves ye," she said gently as she grabbed William's hand, placing it in Kari's small hands. "Live with William and be whole once more. Be with him forever. This is what I am offering the two of you. Forever. Eternity to love. Let me show ye both a life ye have never known."

There was nothing else to say.

William knelt beside Kari, talking to her in only a way he could. "I want this," he said, looking at their joined hands. "Ye are the only woman I want in my bed for all of eternity. Ye are the reason I live and breathe, and I want forever with ye," he said as he caressed her hands.

"Forever," she whispered.

"Aye, my love. Are ye sure?"

"Aye, William," she murmured as she turned back to Serena. "I wish ye to change me, Serena. I will have forever with my William."

" 'Tis settled then," said Seumas.

"I have to be honest with all of ye. I prayed for this. I prayed for a true family, and now, I have found it. I am no longer alone in my wandering of this earth. Thank ye for becoming my family. I promise to keep ye safe and close to my heart at all times. With that said, I have but one more question. When would ye like to do this?" she asked.

"As soon as it can be done, Serena," Kari said, holding a deep affection in her voice. "When do ye suppose we can convert?" she asked, not able to hide her enthusiasm.

William smiled wide at his woman. This was exactly the reason he had fallen in love with her. She was full of surprises. He'd expected her to resist the offer. But she had astonished them all by her quick acceptance. He could not hide his smile, and he did not want to try. Soon enough, they would have forever.

"Soon enough. Mayhap in two to three days. Ye both need time to get yer affairs in order. Make sure that all yer obligations are taken care of. We do not want any looking for ye during the change."

Chapter Thirty One

Seumas took advantage of Serena's moment of silence. As he swiftly repositioned his hold on her body cradling her in his arms, he bounded to his feet and headed for the stairs. He'd had more than enough sharing of his wife, and he did not feel like obliging them any longer.

A few were fast enough to recover from the abrupt leaving to make remarks in between their laughter.

"Well, my warrior, ye have ensured that all shall be talking about this day," she said as she nuzzled his neck.

The rumble she felt in his chest only added to her pleasure.

"Ah... a man wants his wedding day to be remembered," he about growled in her ear.

The feel of her fangs rubbing on his flesh caused his manhood to instantaneously become rock hard. It was not that he wanted to sexually dominate her. No, he wanted more than just coupling. It was the promise of her blood that had him ready to beg for it if he had to. And he knew he would if his mistress wanted to come out and play.

Neither of them thought once the door closed behind them. There they stayed, and not one living soul disturbed them. Food was brought and left on the side table outside their chamber door. None even so much as rapped on the door to demand entrance. Spending three blissful days in each other's arms, and they knew it was at an end.

During the time spent together, they fed, made love, and talked about returning to her time. It was together that they figured out the mystery. The crystal did not only show you what was in man's heart. Once the blade and the crystal joined together, it opened a door. A door that would take them through time—they were sure of it. The blade was the key to returning her to her time in her modern Henderson. Soon, they would see how it worked. First things first—the turning of William and Kari.

"Come, wife. Let us leave our chamber and see our people," he said, holding out his hand.

Serena slipped her hand into his as he led them out of their room and into the corridor and back to the world of the living so to speak. The buzz of the keep came to life. Whispers and heartbeats and the moans of some slammed hard into their senses. The full force of it did not hit them until that moment. Behind their chamber door, nothing else had mattered but the two of them. The noise had drowned out until nothing but their heartbeats existed.

As they walked the keep hand in hand, greeting all who came across their path. Kinsmen and clansmen alike shared blessings with them. All the while placing hands over her womb, praying their lord's seed had taken hold. Even as long as she had lived, a blush still graced her cheeks. She had not been this fondly handled by so many in a very long time.

Seumas saw the blush grace her cheeks and could not help thinking how charming she looked. She was more his century than hers. She had told him of her time and the people that graced the lands. He listened to her talk about all manner of things that he had nay idea what they were. Not only did she talk about them, but she also explained in great detail what the people were truly like and what they all held dear. Items such as cellular phones, iPads, Apple watches and the uses of such items. No longer did people converse with one another, instead found themselves immersed in technology never making eye contact even as they sat at the same table. All that she had told him and what he knew of her, she did not belong in her time. Nay, she suited his century, and his century suited her, right down to the flowing gowns. 'Tis nay the time to ponder on it, nay matter how much he loved to take off her gowns. Time to head outside and face the sunlight.

The keep's doors opened wide, letting the sunlight in. The sun did little to Serena but warm her flesh, but Seumas was a different story. As he was newly turned, his skin would not handle the sunlight well as hers did. But her blood now flowed in his veins. All she could do was cross her fingers and pray. Her blood was old and strong, but it had mutated. It was that mutation that now allowed her to walk freely under the sun without repercussion.

She knew he could withstand the sun, but for how long? They neglected to time how long his body could prolong his duration in the sun. On the day of their wedding, he had limited exposure to fully understand how his body would react. They needed to stay close to the keep's doors in case he required a quick retreat.

"Do nay worry, wife. All shall be well," he murmured next to her ear.

"I pray ye are right. I do not think I will be able to live without ye, husband," she said, looking deep into his eyes.

"Let us step out from the keep for but a moment. Let's see what the day brings us," he said with a smile, the tips of his fangs barely showing. "Come, lass. We'll stay close."

Taking a deep breath and sending a silent prayer to the heavens, her warrior showed no apprehensiveness. Like a true warrior, he conquered all which lay before him. To him, the sun was a foe to be conquered. Triumph he would.

Seumas knew what she feared, and he understood that fear. He had never let trepidation halt him from moving forward, and he would not start now. Yet he was not unwise. He would take precaution and stay close to the door. He was still not sure himself on how his skin shall react to the sunlight. He had done well the day of his wedding, yet there was still a slight tingle on his flesh. A tingle he had not wanted to turn to burned flesh.

Serena felt a shudder of relief surge through her body the moment they stepped back into the privacy of their chamber. A strong urge came over her, and she fought to beat it down. She did not desire to have Seumas feel like a child. But the urge to strip him out of his garments and run her hands over his skin rode her hard.

Every second, every minute spent in the sun had been a stake to the heart. She could have died a thousand times over as more and more clansmen came up to them, wishing them a long and happy life.

Serena's body demanded time to ease the tension. Time was not something she had on her side at the moment. Soon, William and Kari would be at their door, begging for entrance. Together, they'd go through the change. The question now was, who or what were they going to feed on? An animal would have to do. She could not have each person transforming draining their own clansmen.

Seumas would have to help her drain them. She had not fasted, so to speak, to be able to drain two full-grown adults dry. Then, there was the giving of vamp blood to complete the transformation. The blood that would form a bond between the giver and the receiver, a bond tying them together, each knowing where the other was, like a modern-day GPS of sorts.

Serena knew that only her blood would do. Seumas was too newly converted, to have William's and Kari's needs thrust upon him. Her blood shall course through their veins. She shall be the creature of this coven and all loyal to her and her alone.

The knock on their chamber door demanded her attention.

Chapter Thirty Two

Weeks passed since the turning of William and Kari. All had gone well that night, and a sense of calm surrounded them. All had been set right. The actions she had taken were meant to happen. Serena rolled the dice and won against the odds. Fate had shown her cards to be in their favour.

She would return to her century with the help of her friends. They tested their theory of the blade, and to her delight, a portal opened. It had taken some time for them to figure out how to get to where they wanted to go. Serena almost choked on her food when the answer came to her. She could have slapped herself for being so stupid. The answer had been staring at them in the face the whole time. What was in man's heart—that was the answer they sought. That only left them with one more question. Where did the ring fit into all of this? Seumas did not know.

It was apparent that his uncle had not told him all. There was the slight possibility that even he had not known the entire truth about what the crystal did. She was not ready to put all of her apples in that one basket, so to speak. He told her a great deal about his uncle, and he sounded like a man that would know all about what he sought. And it was that knowledge that angered her warrior. He had spent part of his life searching for the crystal and did not know its true purpose. She could not let him be angered with his dead uncle. No use being vexed at the dead. All it got ye was a headache. She would not have him thinking poorly of his uncle.

"I'm quite sure he had no idea of its true purpose. He, like ye, spent his life scouring the land for any trace, any clue that might lead him to the crystal. The blade and the ring as ye know he found first on his many excursions, both were held by different men. I believe yer uncle thought those pieces would lead him to the crystal itself. Whereas ye did not know the blade and the ring had anything to do with the crystal until yer ring drew near the crystal itself. To be honest with ye, I do not think any truly knew its true intention."

"I am inclined to agree with ye, lass. Everything my uncle was, a deceiver was not one of them. He had never in his life told a falsehood. Ye could count on him without fail to be brutally honest. He knew nay other way to be. Yet I find meself wishing he were here now. I can almost see his face and the joyful light that would be in his eyes. He would have loved ye, wife," he said, caressing her cheek.

"Enough of this. Let us figure out the role the ring plays. I do nay think the ring insignificant."

"Nor do I. It, too, has some importance. Mayhap we should put them all together and see what happens."

"Ye are right; we need to put them together simultaneously to see the reaction. When the blade and the crystal join, a door of some sort is opened. We now know to get where ye wish to go is in the holder's heart. Shall we see what will happen, my love?" he said as he escorted her over to the chest, where the items in question were held.

Serena felt her heart rate increase at the mere thought of using it, yet she feared going back to her time. She needed more time in this century. A century that men were men and women were women. Each is defined in life by their gender. Each is happy in life by the role that was set upon them—man with his responsibility as provider and protector and woman with her position as bearer and nurturer. A simple balance between the two genders that modern life did not convey. It had been lost in time, and a very few missed the balance. Even now, with all she knew, it was this time and this place that she would call home.

They might step back into her world for a brief moment in time, but that was all it would be. One brief moment, the past would collide with the future, a future that she would not miss. She wouldn't miss the fast-paced way of life or the information age. Nor would she miss cell phones and text messaging and Starbucks. There was just one thing that she would long for—the few friends she had. But that was easily remedied now that they had the crystal.

Together they would make one quick trip through time to understand how it worked. To make certain they fully comprehended all the risks that may be involved.

"Where should we go, my warrior? Forward in time or back?"

"Let us go back in time. I would like to show ye me, dead wife. If that is all right by ye," he said, gazing tenderly into her eyes. "I know 'tis a lot to ask of ye. I but wish for ye to see the person I was then and the love that I shared with her. For I know now that the love that I had with her was not true love at all but an infatuation. The love I have for ye is born of true and undying love. I would do all in my power to keep ye safe and out of harm's way. Ye shall never feel unwanted or unloved for as long as I may live, and that's going to be for all eternity," he murmured against her lips, placing the gentlest of kisses on her full, inviting mouth. "Tell me ye understand, wife."

"Aye, husband. I more than understand, and I would be honoured if you showed me her. To be perfectly honest with ye, I have wondered about her and the life ye had together," she said as she pierced his flesh, drawing the slightest amount of blood to the surface. The small bead of plasma sitting on his skin called to her. She licked her lips, already able to taste him, and she wanted him.

The look in her eyes and the lift of her chest had him hungering to answer the invitation her body gave off. If they went down this road, they would not be leaving for a very long while. As much as his body demanded he answer her invitation, he could not.

Losing his train of thought, she lapped and suckled his neck, drawing his blood into her. His cock springing to life at the sensation of her lips and tongue moving over his heated flesh, his mind might have wanted to go through time, but the demand from his body rode him harder and he gave into that needed. A primitive growl ripped between them as he turned her around, pushing her down onto the desk. Throwing her gown up onto her back, revealing her feminine curves and the pink folds of her lips.

Holding her in place, he sheathed himself to the hilt of his manhood. He stared at their joined bodies as he moved inside of her. The swell of her mound as her body pulled him back into her wet heated channel. The sight of it drove him to pump harder and faster as he reached for her hair. Pulling on her hair caused her to arch her back, pushing her derrière firmly against him.

Their moans blended together as he worked their bodies. His seed was poised in his shaft, ready to explode at any second. Seumas keeping a tight rein over his urge to blow, not wanting to climax before his lovely wife has reached her peak. She shall have her pleasure before him. His fangs elongated as he felt her body shudder and contract helplessly around his cock. At that moment, he leaned forward, sinking his fangs deep into her exposed neck. Madness coming over him, he thrust urgently behind her, spilling his seed, milking every last spasm and shudder that tore through their bodies.

He did not remember any woman he had been with being as responsive as she was.

She's truly my perfect mate, he thought as he eased their bodies apart. Releasing his hold on her and her gown, he took a step back, allowing her to stand once more.

The smile that graced her face said it all. His woman had no problem with him dominating her. In fact, she absolutely loved it, and so did he. He would be more than happy to dominate her whenever she so wished.

"You may do that to me whenever ye so wish, husband," she purred, placing a kiss on his cheek. "However, I do believe we need to get back to the task at hand, my warrior."

"Aye, my love. We should concentrate on the crystal. Let's see what shall happen." Holding the blade and the crystal in hand ready to step through time. "We shall do this on a three count. Are ye ready, my love?"

"Yes. Let's do this."

"Three. Two. One."

They both held their breath as the blade slid into the centre of the crystal. At the same time, Serena put the ring in place. They watched as it spun one way, then the other, and then stopped. A portal opened and pulled them through. A light flashed before their eyes as it pulled them back in time.

The blur of the light slowed as a panorama view came into sight. Sounds and smells suspended in the air as the portal opened once more. Their bodies slammed back into the world. Their breath came out in puffs of white clouds before them as pieces of snow floated by them as they stepped out of the portal door.

Newly fallen snow covered the ground, reflecting the glow of the fire. Bodies gathered around the fire, seeking warmth. Their jesting and laughter livened the souls of all around on this cold winter night. Laughter filled the air and the hearts of all. They listened and watched the men gathered around the fire and the pure joy that radiated from their faces.

"Come, my love. Let us go inside and seek what it is that brought us here."

"Is it safe, Seumas? Will we not be seen by others? There are now two of ye here."

"Nay worry, wife. I remember this day well. I sent all in the keep home to be with their families. Only a few stayed behind. Nay family to go to. But if ye wish, we could use the power of speed," he said with a little glint in his eyes. "I will carry ye to where we are going," he whispered in her ear as he inhaled her scent. Lifting her into his arms, he made his way to the solar.

He paused outside the door, listening for any possible sound that could be lurking behind the door. All quiet within, as he'd prayed. They were going to slip inside and hide in his secret chamber. A chamber he never told his dead wife about, not wanting to explain its contents. But he had nothing to fear with Serena; he told her all.

"Are we heading to your secret chamber, husband?"

"Aye. 'Tis the only way for ye to watch without us being seen."

Safely in his chamber, they awaited his past self to enter the solar with his dead wife. A wife Serena found herself to be more curious about than she realised. She never had been jealous over other women before. Something about Seumas brought out the little green monster in her. The only thing she chalked it up to was, he was her true mate. A mate she was not willing to share with any other woman, and she'd never have to.

Seumas felt her thoughts as if they were his own. His wife did not have to worry; he did not want any other. He did not blame her for the way she felt. The same emotions ran through him. She would never have need of any other man.

The sounds of Seumas's voice and the voice of a female grew closer. Serena pushed open the peephole, desperate to get a look at the woman. An urgent desire to discover what their relationship was like. Had he doted on her every whim, her every desire or had his eyes wandered from time to time? All thoughts stopped as she saw fire-red hair walk into the chamber. Her voice held a musical note to it, like wind chimes whispering in the wind. There was a grace about her, a confidence that exuded from her very being and radiated around her. She was a nymph. Her warrior had loved a nymph.

There was love in his eyes and something else. She just could not put her finger on it

Chapter Thirty Three

'Tis time to cease this purgatory, lass. The portal beckons," he said as he tugged her into his embrace. Seumas knew full well what was about to happen in the next chamber and he did not want to have his beautiful Serena watch him pleasure his now-dead wife.

"Do ye not wish to stay longer, love?"

"Nay, love. We have been here long enough. Come."

"As ye desire, but catch me if ye can," she said as she bolted out into the open, leaving a breeze in her wake.

He threw his head back, laughing, following her scent as he gave chase. Tracking her to the edge of the portal, where she stood, gazing up at the heavens. Snowflakes blanketed her hair, glistening in the moonlight, like hundreds of tiny gems. He was unable to make himself move, unable to take his eyes off of her, let alone breathe from the mere sight of her. She was his angel on earth, his gift from the heavens.

His attention was drawn back to the portal door behind his angel, how he would love to stay longer and watch her under the moonlight and the newly fallen snow. That, however, was not in the plan. They needed to get back. They'd already spent a great deal of time here, much longer than he'd thought she would want to be. Yet his wife could not seem to take her eyes off of him and his first wife.

The words the *first wife* sent chills down his spine. How he would love to be able to say he had never been married, that Serena was his first and only wife. That simply was not the case.

"Husband," she purred in his mind.

"Aye, love."

"I do not mind that I am yer second wife. I am, however, yer first true mate, as ye are mine. I have wandered for over nine hundred years to find you. Now that I have ye, I do not care if I were yer fifth or sixth wife. For I know that I am and shall always be your first true mate."

"Ye honour me with that knowledge, wife. To me, ye'll always be the one and only. Let us leave this time. We shall be missed soon."

With that, they were gone. Passing through time once more, pulled back to all they'd left behind. The fire light set the portal door aglow. They felt the warmth of the flames touch their flesh as it fought off the bitter cold.

Their chamber never looked so good to her. Her presence, her touch was in everything around them in their chamber, they had not been married long, and still, it felt like home. In all of her wandering, no place ever truly felt like home. There was always something missing. Now that she'd found it, she would not let it go. One more item of business to take care of, and then she could call the keep home for all eternity.

Together, the four of them would travel forward in time to Henderson, Nevada. A century she did not want to go back to, even for the briefest of moments. Go back she would, to make sure the Heffernan's knew she was safe. She couldn't live in Seumas's world without ensuring her dear friends had all they needed.

Seumas gave her gold-and-gem-encrusted dirks she intended to sell. The funds from the sell put in a bank under the Heffernan name. They shall be taken care of once she was gone. That was the least she could do for the people she called friends and family. Though she would rather bring them back.

"Milord, milady."

"Ah, William and Kari are here, love," he said, grabbing her attention.

"Good. Let them in. We have much to discuss with them," she said as she placed the crystal and blade back into the chest, the ring back on Seumas's finger. Not wanting all the pieces in the same place.

"I agree with ye, wife. They should not be all together. We'll move them to our secret chamber at once. Together, we will place a safeguard, a spell of sorts."

"Very wise, husband. No telling who might want to get their hands on the crystal. First, we need to pass the information on to William and Kari."

With that said, she dropped the connection between them as the chamber door burst open.

"Serena, milady, ye are all right," Kari said as she squeezed Serena in a fierce hug. "Ye were here, then ye were gone. I could nay feel ye any longer. I was so worried about ye both," she said as she looked over at Seumas. "What happened? Where did ye go? Ye used the portal, didn't ye?" she about shouted from her excitement.

"Easy, sweetling," murmured William. "They shall tell us in but a minute. I apologise for that, milady."

"Nay worry, William. We should've told ye we were going to use the portal. I did not think about the connection Kari and ye have to Serena. It will not happen again."

"I did not mean to make ye both worry over us. It was meant to be a quick trip back to the past. Time got away from me. You do not have to worry about the next time. For the both of ye shall be joining us," she said with a smile.

Seumas and Serena explained it all to them. Told them about how the crystal worked. How it truly worked. The pieces of the crystal by themselves are harmless enough. The heart of the gem gave the ability to see into man's heart, to see what was desired. Yet, the ring and blade was the key to it all, when brought in close proximity to the piece of the crystal it awakened, allowing for one to travel through time.

Serena told them what to expect once back in her century. Stressing the point that Seumas and William would have to wait in her apartment until she brought them clothes. She could not have them strolling down the Strip in their thirteenth-century Highland garb. More heads would turn than she would like. As it was, the two of them were going to create quite a scene. Women turned their heads as they walked by, some compelled to follow in an attempt to throw themselves at them. Men fighting rage as a fierce resentment struck home. Envious of their mere existence and the power they exuded.

"Can we not go to your time now, Serena? How I do wish to see it for meself," said Kari, unable to hide her enthusiasm any longer. "Even though I fear what ye have told us, I can nay wait to see it. Can ye imagine what it would be like seeing such a sight for the first time?"

Serena could see the elation in their eyes, and she did not blame them. She'd felt the same when she first saw the Vegas lights light up the night sky. But it was more than that. The Vegas strip was its own living being. You could feel the energy the minute ye stepped foot in the casinos. Everything was infused with life, and it was that same life that overflowed onto the Strip's sidewalks. That same energy coursed through the people. Souls that had been drawn to Vegas for the entertainment the nightlife offered. That was not the only draw to Vegas; legal prostitution played a big part. Men and women alike flocked to brothels in an attempt to drop their inhibitions. Very few were able to accomplish what they sought. So, yes, she completely understood the anticipation one could feel when faced with a new environment.

Why should they wait for another day? They now knew how the portal worked, so why not use it now? They could put the crystal and blade in the secret chamber once back from the future. Serena turned to say so to Seumas but did not get to finish that thought, the look on his face told her he knew what she was thinking.

"I know what ye are thinking, lass. Ye are right. There's nay better time than now," he said as he kissed the top of her head. "Gather what ye shall need, my friends. For we leave in twenty minutes."

"At once, milord, milady."

Kari jumped to her feet with an ear-piercing screech as she headed for the door. They all seemed to shake their heads at the same time as they smiled in the wake she had left behind. She was like a newborn fawn discovering the world. In a way, she was. Kari had yet to truly live until now, and she was taking off with a running start. They watched as William followed his mate, and they could not help but laugh.

Before they knew it, they stood in the middle of a clearing. She knew this place and knew it well—Mt. Charleston. They were back where it had all started. Somehow, they needed to make their way back to Tommy and Kimmie's house without being seen. How was she going to get in the house without her friends seeing her, not wanting them to see her just yet? Not yet ready to explain her manner of dress or the husband she now claimed. Serena needed, no required more time to think of a way to make them understand without them thinking she lost her mind. The last thing she desired was to end up in an insane asylum.

Seumas looked around and at once knew this spot. This was where he had first seen his Serena for those few sweet moments before she disappeared. He was not in his world any more, and he would have to defer to his wife for instructions.

Making their way silently to the cabin, they found themselves huddled behind the shrubs.

"Okay, I am going to go inside and get my keys. Wait here. I'll be right back." Sending up a prayer, she moved toward the back door.

Stopping just outside the door, she opened her senses as she scanned the house. No one was home, thank God. She did not have to look or find her keys. She knew exactly where she had left them. Heading straight for her keys, she glanced around the room. No time to wonder where her friends were. The babies! Maybe she was giving birth. She would find out soon enough, but not today.

"Come. We need to get to my place. We need to change. We stand out like sore thumbs," she said over her shoulder as she headed to her car.

How she had missed her Camaro, and she'd give it up willingly for Seumas. Then again, she could sell it and put the money to good use.

"Get in. We have a little bit of a drive to get to my home," she said as she opened the car door and pushed forward the car seat for them to get in.

Once satisfied that they were all buckled in, she threw the car in reverse, spun the wheel, and shifted into gear. They took off like a bat out of hell down the mountain. She went through the gears, shifting and downshifting as she raced down the mountain, making her way to the freeway. As she weaved in and out of traffic, passing cars and trucks alike, not once stepping on the breaks.

Seumas watched with pride as his wife managed the machine with impressive skill. He gazed out the glass at the passing buildings and lights. Lights that lit up the night sky—a sky where he could not see the stars. Not that one would be looking up with all of this to look upon.

"We're here," she said with a sigh as she parked.

It felt like a lifetime since she had been here. Her apartment was small, and it felt even smaller with the four of them in it. They were no longer in the keep, and she already felt the difference. They had work to do, and she wanted to do it fast. The sooner they finished, the sooner they could return home

Chapter Thirty Four

Weeks flew by as they awaited the auction. In that time, Seumas and William mastered her world. Like true warriors, they conquered all in their path. These men were the true meaning of man, no in between with them. Ye either put yer whole heart into what ye sought, or ye might as well have never tried. But these men did not know the meaning of relinquishing of not succeeding in everything they did, a true warrior through and through.

That night, they found themselves at the doors of the Velvet Wings. They made their way to the corner booth and the privacy it offered. The club buzzed with humans and their immortal hosts. The orchestra played, sending yummy vibrations through the humans, causing their blood to awaken. The aroma in the air spoke of their wants, needs, and deepest yearnings. Drawing the immortal to them with those same desires. Desires that spoke of the soul, however dark it might be.

Serena heard her name called over the orchestra's murmur by a familiar voice. A voice she would never miss in any time or century. Rick. Before she knew it, he stood before her, his tall, lanky form blocking her way. Gazing at her as if she had returned from the underworld, having battled Hades himself and lived to talk about it. Rick embraced her in a fierce hug, then held her at arm's length, still unable to believe his eyes.

"I thought they killed you," he said as he pulled her back into his arms. Hugging her a little too tight. "You have not been in, in a very long time. They came looking for you every day until they realised you were not around. I am so glad you are okay."

Serena did not need to know who they were. There were only two choices it could have been. She had guessed they would come looking for her when she did not make her appointment at the Wine Barn. Exactly how long had she been gone?

"Was it the doctor's staff who came for me or the Holy Order?" There was no need to ask any further by his reaction. "It was the Holy Order that came. Wasn't it?"

"Yeah, it was those bastards. They have been searching everywhere for you without success."

She must have been gone longer than she had realised for the Holy Order to come searching for her. Then again, they would have been sent out for her, no matter how short or long a time she was gone. Testing was missed, and she fell off the grid, so to speak. She had expected to come back to Kimmie, Tommy, and their babies. But not to the Holy Order and their minions. This could be very bad. No, she had nothing to fear. There was no way for the Holy Order to find her, the microchips no longer able to send a beacon to her captures. Long ago, it'd turned to dust, and that knowledge offered her peace of mind.

We're safe, she thought with a sigh of relief.

A growl pierced the air as strong hands pulled her back to his side. The air around them filled with male fury as Seumas saw red.

"Take ye filthy hands off of me wife," he snarled, bearing his fangs. All the signs of a true mate showed as he advanced on the barkeep. Only a mate had the right to touch a mate in such a way. "Go to William now," he barked, not taking his eyes off of the other man.

The male's blood was going to be spilled that night for daring to touch his Serena.

"Her ladyship is not to leave Kari's side. Understood, William?" he said firmly for only him to hear.

"Aye, milord."

"Seumas, no. He did not mean anything by his actions. He was concerned for me—that's all," she pleaded with him as William pulled her next to Kari.

"Nay move, milady. Ye are not to interfere. That is yer husband's wish. Kari makes sure she stays by ye side, sweetling."

William knew well that if his ladyship wished to intervene, he could not stop her. She was his maker, and her will was his will. There would be nay stopping her. All he could do was help her.

Serena knew nothing could be done. It was Seumas's right as her mate to draw blood when dishonoured. And dishonoured he had been. In their world, there was no need for rings to mark one's mate. If it was a true mating, more than a bond was formed. Ye became marked with yer mate's scent, a silent warning to all males and females alike, a warning that should have registered with Rick. But it didn't, and now, he would pay the price for his folly. Perhaps he had spent far too long in this modern time—hell, in this city for that matter—that he'd forgotten the old ways. As so many of them had. They had all disregarded the ancient ways along with all the other rights, all in an attempt to fit in with the humans and the world they had created.

Guilt hit her as both men moved forward in acceptance of the age-old rights. The whole club seemed to cease what they were doing. As all the humans were escorted out and off of the club's premises. Keeping the humans and the secrets of the race safe. Blood would be drawn this night and honour regained.

Rick and Seumas circled one another as the crowd pushed in eagerly to witness the age-old ritual. Growls came from both males as they charged each other. She watched at Kari's side as William moved forward through the crowd, ready to assist his lord.

She felt every punch and tear of flesh as if it were her own. Blood seeped out from every cut made and every punch thrown, staining their clothes crimson, bodies healed seconds later leaving no trace of injury. The crimson stains are the only evidence of a well-placed strike. She watched in complete horrification, yet at the same time completely fascinated by the two men facing off.

A roar cut through the clamour of all gathered. Bodies flew toward the walls of the club as Rick impacted with them. Seumas stood in the middle of the now half-circle, his chest expanding with every breath that he took. His broad shoulders were hunched over, his head lowered, his eyes fixed on his target as he slowly stalked Rick. A true predator showing no sign of mercy for his prey, he had only one thing on his mind—the need to end this man's life.

To all of their surprise, he stopped short of his target. He gazed down at the now-limp form. Something changed within him. The fire that blazed in his eyes dimmed, and in its place was empathy. Blood had been spilled and honour restored. But there was no honour in leaving this man unconscious on the dirty club floor. Seumas lifting him with great ease into the nearby booth. Once satisfied the male would be taken care of, he took his leave.

Holding out his hand, he said, "Come, love. Let us go home. I do nay wish to share ye any more this night."

"Yes, my love. Let us go home," she whispered as her eyes briefly gazed over to where Rick lay, still unconscious.

For the briefest of seconds, she wanted to check on him, needing to make sure he still lived. There was nothing to be done and she knew it well. If he was dead, she could not bring him back. Game over. All she could do was have hope in his will to live.

The thought of Rick lying in that booth crossed her mind from time to time as the auction drew near. She had a sense of guilt that she could not shake, that too would pass. Guilt was not to her liking and soon they'll be back in a century that she understood. They all seem to be counting the days until they return to the safety of the keep.

Auction day was finally upon them and she could feel the energy vibrating within her. Energy desperate to bust free of its capture, she could not seem to be still. Pacing the length of her apartment's living room she awaited the call from the auction house. A phone call which would change all for the Heffernan household and hers, a great deal of money was going to be made this day, but how much had yet to be known.

A smile settled upon her lips as she recalled the look on the auctioneer's face. A look of complete shock and utter enthusiasm crossed his very expressive features. It had taken a few minutes for him to catch himself and come back to his senses. The enjoyment in his eyes shone bright.

She found amusement in the way he stuttered and stumbled over words as he tried explaining the objects in his hands. They acted as if they did not know anything about the items he held. The estimate given was much more than they had anticipated. A great deal of money, which could very well go over the estimated amount.

"Wife, cease pacing. Ye are making me dizzy. Come sit with me," he murmured as he moved to make room for her next to him.

Their time here was almost over, and he wanted one more memory of her in her century. They'd taken moonlit walks and talked about all sorts of things. One conversation stuck out beyond any other. His lovely wife, his beautiful Serena, wanted children. God... he could only hope she carried his bairn already. The heavens knew he had been working hard on fulfilling her desire for children. He was more than up to the task right now, his proof straining against his jeans. Seumas shifted in his seat in a vain attempt to adjust, not wanting to force his hunger on her. Coupling was not what she needed and not what he truly craved. He wanted nothing more than to feel her warmth against him.

Serena cuddled close to her husband as she let herself relax, slowly drifting to sleep's embrace. He stroked her hair with such tenderness that it warmed her heart. He knew what to do to help her relax and ease her worries.

"Rest, mistress. Sleep now. I'll wait for the call. Then, we shall go home, love," he said as he placed a kiss on the top of her head.

"Home," she murmured as sleep claimed her.

"Aye, love. Home and the beginning of our life together."